"What do you thin

here?"

"One grave. I'm a bit confused about the location."

"What do you mean?" Colt asked.

Jordyn pointed to the edge of the graveyard in the distance. "The cemetery ends over there."

"You're thinking criminal activity?"

"Possibly." She picked up her bag. "I want to photograph the perimeter to get a clear picture of the scene."

"I can't leave you to do that alone." Colt tugged on Bones's leash.

"I realize my dad called you in, but I'll be fine. Besides, you and the other constables are nearby." She didn't wait for a reply and made her way across the property.

A flicker in the balsam firs caught her eye. *What is that?* She squatted for a better look.

Bones barked somewhere behind her.

A shot rang out, dirt flying at her feet.

"Jordyn! Get down!" Colt's cry came as another shot pierced the early-morning air.

As she dove to the ground, covering her head with her hands, a thought arose.

She'd found a grave someone wanted to keep hidden.

Darlene L. Turner is an award-winning author who lives with her husband, Jeff, in Ontario, Canada. Her love of suspense began when she read her first Nancy Drew book. She's turned that passion into her writing and believes readers will be captured by her plots, inspired by her strong characters and moved by her inspirational message. Visit Darlene at www.darlenelturner.com, where there's suspense beyond borders.

Books by Darlene L. Turner

Love Inspired Suspense

Border Breach
Abducted in Alaska
Lethal Cover-Up
Safe House Exposed
Fatal Forensic Investigation
Explosive Christmas Showdown
Alaskan Avalanche Escape
Mountain Abduction Rescue
Buried Grave Secrets

Visit the Author Profile page at LoveInspired.com.

BURIED GRAVE SECRETS

DARLENE L. TURNER

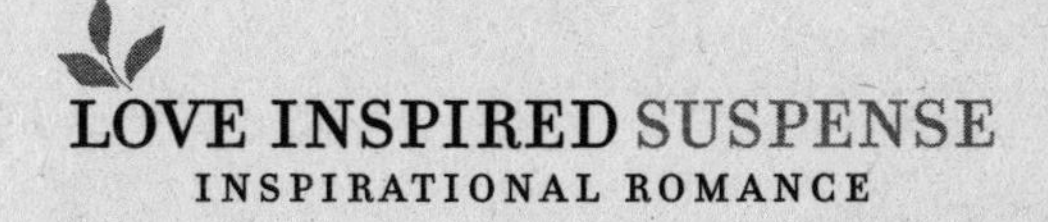

Recycling programs for this product may not exist in your area.

ISBN-13: 978-1-335-59925-4

Buried Grave Secrets

For questions and comments about the quality of this book, please contact us at CustomerService@Harlequin.com.

Love Inspired
22 Adelaide St. West, 41st Floor
Toronto, Ontario M5H 4E3, Canada
www.LoveInspired.com

Printed in U.S.A.

Then spake Jesus again unto them, saying,
I am the light of the world: he that followeth me shall
not walk in darkness, but shall have the light of life.
—*John* 8:12

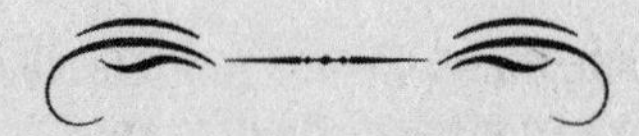

For DiAnn Mills
Your mentorship shaped my writing journey. Thank you.
Redheads rock!

Acknowledgments

My Lord and Savior, thank You for Your blessings and goodness. Help me to always *shine* for You!

Jeff and my sissy Susan, I couldn't do this without your support. Thanks for believing in me when I struggle with my own inadequacies. I love you both very much.

Dr. Janna Andronowski, thank you for helping me understand the world of forensic anthropology. I appreciate you taking time to video chat with me and answering my many questions. Anything I embellished for fiction is totally on me.

My agent, Tamela Hancock Murray, thanks for your continued guidance in my writing journey.

My editor, Tina James. I love working with you. Thank you for making my stories shine!

Darlene's Border Patrol, thank you for reading my books and helping spread the word. I'm thankful for the friendships we've developed!

My readers, I'm grateful for your support. Thank you for reading my books.

ONE

A dark, creepy graveyard. Not how forensic anthropologist Dr. Jordyn Miller wanted to start her day. However, she had no choice. After receiving an anonymous tip, police had found an unmarked grave along the tree line at the edge of her town, Charock Harbour, Newfoundland. Jordyn needed to examine the bones at the scene before an approaching hurricane hit her region. Storms on the Rock were devastating, and she couldn't have any evidence destroyed.

Flashing lights from the police cruisers and the crime scene forensic van parked in the Charock Cemetery lot, along with raised spotlights stationed around the site, announced their presence. If the nearby neighbors hadn't already been awake, they would be by now, and soon a crowd would form—even in the early morning. She knew how most residents in small towns liked to talk. It was only a matter of time before word spread about the mysterious discovery in their community of twenty thousand. Time to get to work.

Jordyn ducked under the yellow caution tape and clicked on her flashlight, catching a glimpse of a skeleton in its beam. She headed toward the crime scene investigator who'd called the chief medical examiner and requested Jordyn's presence at the scene. Since the site was near her home, she'd arrived immediately. At five in the morning, darkness still blanketed the region, and the gruesome sight before her sent chills slithering down Jordyn's spine. She stopped in her tracks and moved the light over the mound of soil beneath a balsam fir. Even though she was accustomed to bones, her gut churned at the mystery surrounding the grave.

"Thanks for getting here so quickly." A male police officer approached and stuck out his gloved hand. "I'm fairly new to the team. Constable Harley Lavigne." He gestured to a female officer scouring the property. "Constable Sara Greer and I have secured the site for you." He paused. "Wait, you're the premier's daughter, aren't you?"

Jordyn cringed. Why did people always associate her with her father? She'd made a name for herself within the forensic community. However, the Honorable Russell Miller had just been reelected and demanded their entire family celebrate in the limelight, which meant she'd had to spend time with her twin sister, Morgan, and her husband, Tyler—Jordyn's ex-fiancé. It had been years since their betrayal, but it still felt like yesterday.

"I'm *Dr.* Jordyn Miller." She couldn't resist emphasizing the word *doctor.* "Sorry, I don't shake hands while working. You understand." Truth be told, her colleagues often teased her over her fear of bugs since she had to both dig in the soil—which was full of creepy-crawly creatures—*and* clean the bones at the Health Sciences Centre in Charock Harbour, close to the university, where she taught. The office of the chief medical examiner had appointed her to lead a unit in their work across the province. Part-time professor, part-time forensic anthropologist; it was the best of both worlds. "Thank you for sending over your police photos. I appreciate it." She had reviewed them carefully before arriving at the site.

A white news van drove into the cemetery lot, and a female reporter exited.

Great. That was all they needed. Now word about a hidden grave on the outskirts of town would be blasted into every home.

"Of course." The constable stuffed his hand in his pocket. "Our team has finished with the scene. It's all yours." He gestured toward the approaching reporter. "I'll keep them at bay. You do your investigation."

"Thank you. We can't have anyone contaminating the scene." Jordyn walked over to the mound of soil and inspected the grave. A full skeleton lay exposed in the dirt. No coffin. Odd. She squatted and set her bag down, peering back toward the parking lot.

Constable Lavigne raised his hands to block the reporter from advancing any farther. Constable Greer joined him as more onlookers tried to advance past the caution tape.

With them in control, it was time to examine the scene.

Jordyn withdrew her sketch pad and pencil, then drew a map of the area. Over the next couple of hours, she documented the grave and took pictures of the site as much as she could in the dark. She'd learn for sure whether this person had died of natural causes or something more sinister after providing her findings to Dr. Vance Chambers, their medical examiner.

Her cell phone chimed, and she fished it out of her bag. Her father.

Watch your back. Got a threat against your life. Sending protection your way.

What? Really, Dad? I don't need your help.

Their shaky relationship had come to a head recently when she'd questioned him about a childhood memory that had resurfaced a few months before. He had told her to leave it alone, but she couldn't shake the feeling that she'd buried an important event from years ago.

She typed a reply.

I'm fine. Why would anyone threaten me?

She waited for a response.

Something about getting out of his graveyard.

She tensed and glanced around the property. How did anyone know she was there? She observed the reporter's van, and suspicion prickled the hairs on her arms.

The constables on site will keep me safe. Gotta get to work.

Another ding.

Get in your car and wait for protection.

Not happening, Dad. I have a job to do. Jordyn resisted the urge to mumble out loud and stuffed her phone back into her bag, then snapped it closed.

Moments later, squealing tires caught her attention, and she pushed herself to her feet.

An East Newfoundland Constabulary SUV

with the words *K-9 Unit* on the back flew into the parking lot.

Jordyn held her breath as the vehicle's door opened. *Please don't let it be him.*

Constable Peters stepped out.

Jordyn's shoulders slumped. *Thanks, Dad.*

Her father just *had* to send the man who'd broken her heart as her protection detail. However, she knew the reason why. Constable Colt Peters's protector and patrol dog was one of the best.

Colt had been training his German shepherd, Bones, since he was a puppy. Jordyn had fallen in love with both the dog and his handler almost immediately. After Tyler's betrayal, she'd never thought she'd love again, but Colt's personality had made it so easy.

A mistake she'd regretted ten months later, when Colt broke up with her for reasons she still didn't understand. The hole he'd left had been unbearable. Even in their small town, she'd been successful in avoiding him. Leave it to her dad to open that proverbial can of worms.

Colt opened the rear door, and Bones jumped out. Colt attached his leash and headed Jordyn's way.

She walked toward them, as she didn't want the duo close to the grave. "Colt, you didn't have to come."

"And face your dad's wrath? No thank you." He rubbed his K-9's fur. "How've you been?"

"I'm fine. I don't need protection, Colt."

Bones whined and looked up at his handler.

Colt chuckled. "He wants to say hi and is asking my permission." He unhooked the K-9's leash. "Release, Bones."

Jordyn knew that meant Bones was temporarily off duty, so she bent beside the dog and petted his head. "Good to see you, my friend." She eyed Colt. "You too. Hope you've been well."

Colt smiled. "I'm good. Busy."

She resisted the urge to stare at his handsome face and the cute dimple in his chin. Even after ten months, the pain still sliced through to her core.

Bones snuggled closer, as if sensing her feelings, and licked her face with sloppy kisses.

I've missed you, too, bud.

Jordyn suppressed the rush of emotions and stood, noting the growing crowd of curious onlookers. Obviously, word had spread quickly, even on the outskirts of town. "We have to keep these people back. Can you help the constables? I have to finish my preliminary investigation and bring in my team."

"What do you think we're dealing with here?" Colt asked, putting Bones back on his leash.

"One grave. I'm a bit confused about the location."

"What do you mean?"

Jordyn pointed to the edge of the graveyard in

the distance. "The Charock Cemetery ends over there. I understand the funeral home was about to expand their plots, but this grave is still close to the plot line."

"You're thinking criminal activity?"

"Possibly, but I don't like to speculate." She picked up her bag and placed the strap over her shoulder. "I want to photograph the perimeter to get a clear picture of the scene. Once my team arrives with the drone, we'll get a better view. Meanwhile, why don't you help Constable Lavigne?"

"I can't leave you to do that alone." Colt tugged on Bones's leash.

"Look, I realize my dad called you in, but I'll be fine. Besides, you and the other constables are nearby. Trust me, I'm perfectly safe." Instead of waiting for his reply, she turned and made her way across the property. *Dad, you really didn't need to send a babysitter.*

Ugh! She was testy and needed her morning pumpkin spice latte—her seasonal favorite. There'd been no time to stop for one as she'd hurried to get there.

In the glare of her flashlight, Jordyn studied the ground and walked toward the property's tree line. A flicker in the balsam firs caught her eye. *What is that?* She moved to the right and squatted for a better look.

Bones barked somewhere behind her.

A shot rang out, dirt flying at her feet.

"Jordyn! Get down!" Colt's cry came as another shot pierced the early-morning air.

As she dove to the ground, covering her head with her hands, a thought arose…

She'd found a grave someone wanted to keep hidden.

Constable Colt Peters whipped out his SIG Sauer and unleashed his K-9. "Bones, guard!"

Bones bolted toward Jordyn, barking ferociously. He positioned himself in front of her like a sentry guarding their subject.

Another shot echoed throughout the area.

Colt raised his gun and fired toward the tree line, praying for Jordyn's protection. *Lord, keep her safe.* He silently chastised himself for not acting on his instincts to stick closer to her side. Now he'd never hear the end of it from their province's premier—her father.

Colt had his own reasons for saying yes to Russell Miller's call. The site of the skeletal remains was near the area where Colt had left his brother ten years ago after they'd had a huge fight. Colt had seized the opportunity to check out the site for himself. His brother, Linc, had gone missing after a night Colt would never forget—the night his mother stopped talking to him. The night he abandoned his brother. She blamed him for her older son's disappearance. Memories of that night cut through him like a fresh wound. They'd fought about a girl. Colt had confessed how much he liked her but then found Linc kissing her in the college library. Colt's anger had escalated on their drive home, when Linc told him the girl had said she didn't like Colt and only felt sorry for him. Linc had asked her out. Colt had stopped the car and told him to walk the rest of the short distance home. However, he'd never made it home. The guilt had driven Colt to go into law enforcement, and ever since he'd become an officer, he used the resources at his disposal to try to locate Linc, but he'd been unsuccessful. It was as if his brother had simply vanished. Now Colt wanted to learn if the remains that had been found there were Lincoln Peters's.

He hit the button on his radio and called for backup when he reached Jordyn. He crouched beside her. "You okay?"

"I'm fine. Is the shooter gone?" Jordyn raised her head.

Constable Lavigne approached, panting. "What direction did the shot come from? Greer and I were keeping the crowd back."

Jordyn pointed. "I noticed a flash over by the tree line."

"I called it in," Colt told him. "Get Greer to secure the perimeter until other constables arrive. The suspect hasn't fired again, so he's probably gone, but we have to guard Dr. Miller."

"On it." The younger officer raised his weapon and dashed toward the trees.

Colt helped Jordyn stand. "That wasn't smart. You should've stayed close. Seems like your father was correct in asking for my help."

He didn't miss the scowl on her face, but she remained silent.

She knew he was right.

"Let's get you inside your van." Colt turned to his German shepherd. "Bones, guard."

The dog moved closer to the beautiful anthropologist. A long strand of brown hair escaped the hood of her personal protective suit, and Colt resisted the urge to tuck it back in. He also ignored the glare in her narrowed eyes.

"Colt, this attack proves something sinister is going on here." She gestured toward the trees. "That shooter doesn't want me to find anything else, and that tells me there's more."

"More remains, you think?"

"Possibly. I've mapped and photographed the scene, but I'll need the team to bring the rest of our equipment. In the meantime, I'm going to look closer at the grave." She scooped up her bag, which had fallen to the ground when she dove for cover. "If you and Bones want to protect me, you both need to keep your distance. Don't contaminate anything."

He hissed out a breath through his teeth. "You're

still as stubborn as ever." *And as beautiful.* He kept the latter thought to himself.

"*Determined*, not *stubborn*. There's a difference."

He didn't miss her teasing tone before she headed toward the unmarked grave.

Colt pointed to her retreating back. "Bones, heel."

The dog fell in line with Jordyn, staying close but keeping his distance at the same time. Colt followed, still holding his gun. He wasn't taking any more chances—even if it meant he had to remain near the woman he'd once loved with all his heart. The personal reasons he'd broken up with her still haunted him, but it had been for the best. He'd risk his shattered emotions to protect her.

Approaching footsteps jolted him back to the situation, and he pivoted, raising his gun.

Constable Sara Greer lifted her hands. "Just me. Perimeter is secure. No sign of the shooter."

Sirens blared as two cruisers screeched into the parking lot.

"Good job—thanks." Colt noted a security camera mounted on the warehouse for Charock Lighting, which was next door to the cemetery. He turned to Greer and pointed. "Can you ask the sergeant to obtain a warrant for video footage from that camera? It might have caught our perp on tape."

Greer holstered her weapon. "On it. I'll update

the others as well." She jogged toward the additional constables.

Assured the suspect had fled, Colt returned his weapon to his duty belt and approached Jordyn.

She jumped up. "Wait. Don't come any closer." She dug out another suit from her bag and tossed it to him. "Put this on first."

Bones remained nearby, keeping watch.

Colt did as she'd asked, fastening his duty belt on the outside to keep his weapon and communication devices close. He kneeled beside her, eyeing the skeleton. "What are your initial assessments? Male? Female? Young? Old?" Colt knew Jordyn hated to guess and would want to conduct a more thorough examination of the bones, but he was curious to hear her thoughts. Curious if they could be his brother's.

She pointed to the remains. "The pelvic area indicates female. As to the age, I require a closer review in my lab. You know how I need facts before I make conclusions. I can't speculate."

"Understood." Colt exhaled slowly. *Not Linc.* Part of him was relieved, but the other part just wanted to give his family answers.

Jordyn tilted her head and looked at him. "I know what you're thinking. It's not Lincoln, Colt. I realize this is around the area you said you left him, but this skeleton is definitely female." She reached out and squeezed his shoulder.

Colt moved away from her touch. "Thanks for confirming. I was curious."

"You still searching for him?"

"I have to, Jordyn. Mom needs closure, even if she never speaks to me again."

"I understand."

Colt unhooked his flashlight from his belt and shined the beam into the crudely constructed grave, walking around the hole. He stopped. "That's interesting."

"What do you see?"

He studied the bones that lay nestled in the shallow, narrow grave. "I would think cemetery workers would have dug a deeper hole. This looks to me like whoever created this grave did it in a hurry. Plus, there's no coffin."

"I agree, and they put it right under a balsam fir. That tells me they were probably trying to give the grave shelter."

"That's a stretch. How would you know that?"

Jordyn stood and shrugged. "Just a hunch. Perhaps it was a loved one or something."

"Sounds like you're speculating. Doesn't that contradict what you just said? Facts first?"

She huffed but remained silent.

"I'm just kidding." Colt squatted at the head of the hole, shining his light from a different angle. "Wait—what's tucked under the left hand?" He pointed. "I can see an edge of it in the dirt from this viewpoint."

Jordyn moved closer. “Good eye. How did I miss that?” She picked up her brush and dusted the soil from the object in question. “Well, I’ll be.”

“What is it?”

“A wood carving of a lynx. Odd. Why would someone include this in a grave?”

Colt moved his light closer. The rectangular piece of wood held an intricate carving of the Canada lynx. The edges were round and sanded. Someone had carefully burned marks into the image, giving the creature dimension. “A skilled hand did this. Note the detail. Perhaps the killer’s way of replacing a typical tombstone?”

“Maybe—but, Colt, we don’t know how the woman died. Could just be from natural causes, not homicide.”

“Perhaps.” Did she really believe that after just being shot at? The cop in him said otherwise.

Bones pranced around Jordyn, whining.

Colt bristled. Something was wrong. His dog wouldn’t react that way unless he’d sensed some type of danger. “Get behind me, Jordyn.” He clipped his flashlight back onto his belt and removed his weapon. “What is it, Bones?”

The K-9 barked and shot off toward another area of trees.

Jordyn sprinted, following Bones.

“Wait!” Why did she put herself at risk so easily? Colt cringed and raced after the duo.

Jordyn tripped and fell onto a fresh patch of dirt hidden by a tree stump. "Ugh!" she yelled.

Bones barked.

Colt caught up to them, then hauled Jordyn to her feet.

She gasped and pointed.

Close to where she'd fallen, a bony hand protruded from the soil.

TWO

Jordyn's pulse thundered in her head as she surveyed the small, sheltered clearing. The new grave told her one thing—this was probably an unmarked graveyard, with more remains hidden. Since daybreak had dawned, she would request her response-and-recovery task force report to the scene. The team consisted of her trainees and folks who specialized in archaeology. The threat of a hurricane and a determined shooter could try to stop her, but she wouldn't be deterred.

Jordyn straightened her shoulders with conviction. "Colt, I'm calling my team now. They should be in the office. I'm thinking we'll find more graves here. That's what the shooter wanted to hide. We'll get our ground-penetrating radar going."

He pursed his lips for a split second, then said, "I have to get you to safety. You're too exposed. Your father would never forgive me if something happened to you."

She placed her hands on her hips. "I appreciate that, but my father needs to let me do my job—and so do you. We have a serious situation on our hands here."

"And my job is to protect you, Jordyn. Can't your team investigate?"

She raised her cell phone in the air. "Yes, but I have to lead them." Her finger hovered over the speed dial button. "They're fairly new and require direction. You can increase the security by adding more constables, but I need to do this."

Jordyn hated to be difficult, but she had a job to do. The media had been following her ever since she'd accepted the position. Many people had doubted her abilities and accused her father of nepotism. The allegations angered Jordyn. After successfully assisting the medical examiner by giving her findings, she'd helped solve many cold cases, proving her abilities. She couldn't mess up this new case, or the press would hound her even more. She hit the button and walked toward the newest grave while she waited for someone to pick up. It was only seven o'clock, but she knew her team always arrived at the lab early to prep for Jordyn's eight o'clock class. However, today, they would have to cancel her lecture. The new remains took precedence.

"Eve speaking. How may I help you?" The young graduate trainee had started on Jordyn's team six months ago and had already proven herself tenfold.

"Morning, Eve. It's Jordyn. I need you and Nick out at the Charock Cemetery. Bring our equipment and the archeology team. We have a potential site of an unmarked graveyard north of the cemetery's plot line. I've done some mapping and taken photos, but the upcoming storm means we'll have to work quickly. Plus, someone is threatening the area."

"What? Will we be safe?" Eve asked.

"Constables are securing the scene and will protect us." Jordyn rubbed her left temple, hoping to ward off a headache. Time for caffeine. "Can you also pick me up a pumpkin spice latte? It's gonna be a long day, and we'll probably have to work into the night."

Bones bumped against her legs, reminding her of his presence and her predicament. Protection detail provided by her ex-boyfriend. At least Bones hadn't broken her heart.

"Sounds serious," Eve said.

Jordyn didn't miss the angst in her trainee's voice. She didn't know the half of it...yet. "Bring all the usual gear and bags. Something tells me we're gonna need lots of them. Also, cancel today's classes."

Eve whistled. "Not a good start to the week."

"Not at all." Jordyn observed the grave they'd just discovered. She wanted to get a good look before anyone else arrived. “Oh, Eve, bring more PPE suits. I don’t want anyone contaminating anything.”

“Got it. See you soon.” Eve clicked off.

Jordyn’s phone buzzed before she could stuff it back into her bag. She checked the screen and cringed. Her boss, the chief medical examiner. “Dr. Jones, how are you?” With his many bow ties and his fedora, Zechariah Jones reminded Jordyn of a famous television medical examiner.

“Dr. Miller, your father just called me. Why am I hearing from him about another unmarked grave and not you?” His voice held frustration.

Jordyn gripped her phone tighter. *How did Dad find out so quickly?* Right, her father was close friends with the constabulary’s deputy chief of police. “I’m sorry, sir. I was shot at earlier, so it’s been a precarious morning and I haven’t had time to bring you up to speed. The situation has escalated, and the team is en route.”

“What? Are you okay?” His voice had switched from frustration to concern. “Tell me what’s happening.”

The man had always treated Jordyn with respect.

Unlike her own father.

“I’m fine. The constabulary is protecting us. When you called me in, you stated the anonymous tipster said they found one skeleton. I found another one hidden close to the first. The fact that I was shot at tells me someone wants to keep something hidden."

"You mean, more remains?"

"Call it a hunch, but we'll know more once we deploy Greta." The team had nicknamed their portable ground-penetrating radar machine Greta in tribute to a fellow professor who had recently passed. "We'll do our examination and work closely with Dr. Chambers. Put the other medical examiners on standby. Something tells me there's more here to unearth, and we might need their help." Jordyn watched the constables trying to restrain the reporter. Not good. "Sir, the press is here. What do you want me to tell them if they ask?" And she knew they would.

"Just that you have no comment other than you're investigating. Jordyn, be careful. I don't like that you've been shot at. Maybe I should take over."

"I'll be fine." She glimpsed Colt standing nearby, keeping guard. "My father sent me a personal bodyguard and his sidekick K-9, Bones."

At the mention of his name, Bones's ears twitched.

Jordyn resisted the urge to go up and hug the dog, understanding that he was on duty. Colt would remind her not to interfere.

Dr. Jones chuckled. "Now that's an appropriate name."

"Sure is, and he's the best."

Dark clouds now blanketed the sky. "I gotta get going. This is gonna take a while, and we need to get everything into place before the rain storm hits."

"They're also predicting the hurricane is gonna be a doozy, and it's arriving in a couple of days. You best work quickly. Keep me updated." Dr. Jones ended the call.

Jordyn slipped her phone into her bag and approached Colt. Bones followed. "My team is en route. Are extra constables coming?"

"The sergeant approved a few more, but we're a constabulary satellite office and are limited on officers. They're on their way. Plus, he's contacted a judge to get a warrant for the camera next door." He turned in the building's direction. "It's a bit of a distance, but it may still have caught something. Constable Greer has gone to talk to any employees on shift right now."

"Since you have to be by my side, keep your PPE suit on, and let's head back to the new grave. I want to adjust my map to include it and take pictures."

Colt gestured toward the balsam fir. "After you."

Jordyn made her way to their newly discovered grave nestled between two firs and scrutinized it, then added it to her map.

Colt pointed to the protruding finger. "I wonder if there's another wood carving buried with the remains."

Jordyn squatted and examined the area. "Perhaps. We'll know more once we clear the soil."

"I keep wondering about Linc. Could it be him?"

She wiped her forehead with the back of her hand. "Do you really think he's still in the region?"

Colt let out a long exhale. "Not sure."

Jordyn's phone buzzed. "This may be my team." She fished it out and hit Accept without looking at the screen. "Dr. Miller here."

"Jordyn! I think I'm being followed." Her estranged twin sister's frantic voice boomed in Jordyn's ear. "I need your help. Tyler is out of town. Mom and Dad are in an important meeting, so I'm calling you."

Jordyn stood. "Morgan, calm down. Tell me what's going on." Since the betrayal, she rarely spoke to her sister.

"I was taking the kids to school and noticed a white pickup drive into the lot after me." She took a breath. "I didn't think anything of it until I noticed the same truck pull in behind me at my favorite coffee shop."

"Morgan, the town has lots of white pickups."

"Not with the same lynx decal on the hood."

Jordyn stiffened and whipped her gaze over to Colt.

He raised a brow.

Coincidence? Or could the lynx carvings somehow be connected?

Colt's heartbeat spiked at the terror-stricken expression contorting Jordyn's face. Even Bones had reacted to his subject's body language by moving closer. Colt knew she was talking to her twin, Morgan, but what had upset her sister? He grazed Jordyn's arm. "What is it?"

Jordyn pulled the phone slightly farther away. "She thinks someone is following her. A truck with a lynx decal on it."

What? He had to get her protection. "Tell me where she is."

"Morgan, you remember Constable Colt Peters, right? Well, he's here with me. I'm putting you on speakerphone." Jordyn hit a button. "Where are you exactly?"

"Charock Café on Second Street."

Colt inched closer to the phone. "Morgan, it's Colt. Are you inside the building?"

"Yes. When I saw the truck park in the lot, I hurried into the café."

"Did you see the driver? Can you describe him or her?" Colt asked.

"No, the truck has tinted windows, and I didn't wait around."

"Stay inside." Colt unhooked his radio. "I'm sending someone to your location."

"Okay. Jordyn, Dad told me earlier you were involved in an investigation and needed protection. Am I being followed because of you?"

Colt didn't miss the anger that overtook Morgan's voice.

A grave expression engulfed Jordyn's pretty face. "Morgan, we don't know that this is anything yet. I'm simply doing my job."

"Well, your 'job' puts your family in jeopardy."

Her eyes narrowed. "Did Dad tell you that?"

Colt stepped back to distance himself from the sisters' squabble. He hit his radio button and requested a cruiser to Morgan's location.

His cell phone buzzed in his belt clip. He brought it out and checked the screen. A text from Jordyn's father. Great.

Call me.

Colt returned to Jordyn's side. "Morgan, a cruiser is on its way. Remember what I said—stay there and don't go anywhere alone. Not even the bathroom."

"I hope they get here fast. I need to get to work." A voice blared through the speakerphone. "My order is ready. At least coffee will comfort me while I wait. Gotta run."

"You'll be okay, Morgan. I promise. Call again if you want to talk." Jordyn ended the call. "I didn't just lie to my sister, did I?"

"She'll be fine. The constable on duty will protect her. They're aware she's the premier's daughter."

"Why does she always blame me for everything? She acts like *I* betrayed *her*." Jordyn's clenched jaw revealed her frustration.

Colt was well aware of how Morgan had admitted to being in love with Jordyn's fiancé just before Jordyn was ready to walk down the aisle on her wedding day. Morgan and Tyler had been having an affair for three months. The twins' solid bond had been severed ever since. They rarely spoke.

"I'm sorry. It's not your fault, Jordyn." Once again, Colt's cell phone buzzed. He looked at the screen.

Now.

The Honorable Russell Miller meant business. When he spoke, people reacted fast. "I gotta make a call. Will you be okay with Bones? I'll be right over there." He pointed.

"I'll be fine. I want to keep working on the map. My team will be here soon." She moved back to the grave.

"Bones, heel," Colt commanded.

His K-9 followed Jordyn and sat back from her position but close enough to stay on guard.

Just like Colt had trained him. *Good boy.*

Colt punched in the premier's private number and waited.

"About time you called."

Colt counted to five slowly in his head. Jordyn's father had been civil to him when Colt had dated his daughter, but he always had an abruptness to him. Protective of his girls, maybe. However, Colt had sensed something else hindered Russell and Jordyn's relationship. Morgan appeared to be the premier's favorite daughter.

"Sorry, sir. Been a tad busy here."

"So I've heard. Give me an update."

Colt explained the situation, including their plan to provide protection for Morgan.

"My wife and I are coming to stay at our cottage residence," Russell said. "I'm too far away here in St. John's. I'll be contacting the deputy chief and increasing security around my daughters."

"I've already arranged that, sir. Plus, Bones and I will watch Jordyn closely."

"Well, I need more. I will not lose my daughters to whoever is digging around in graveyards. Do we know anything about this shooter?"

"Nothing so far. We're obtaining a warrant for a nearby camera, but we're waiting on Judge Adly."

"I'll get my office to put some pressure on him. You'll have it soon."

Well, I guess it helps to have a father as the

premier after all. "Constables are canvassing the area now, but it's pretty remote out here. I believe the shooter fled into the woods." Colt paused when he noted vans driving into the cemetery's parking lot.

"Sir, if there's nothing more, I have to get going. Jordyn's team has arrived, and I need to talk to them."

"Keep me updated." The man disconnected.

Colt clipped his phone back onto his belt and walked toward an approaching redhead. A man exited the driver's side of the van and moved to the back doors. Additional team members emerged from the other vehicle.

Colt raised his hands to the young woman. "Stop, please. Show me your identification."

The redhead pointed toward Jordyn. "I'm with Dr. Miller."

Colt turned to see Jordyn pop up from her position at the forest's edge and then jog in their direction. "Colt, it's okay. This is Eve Harrison and Nick Elliott. My trainee and research assistant." She gestured toward the additional van. "The others are from our archeology department. They'll assist in our recovery."

"I figured, but your father is watching closely, and I can't make any mistakes in your security detail."

"Your what?" Eve asked Jordyn.

"My dad brought Colt and Bones in to protect

me." Jordyn gestured toward his dog. "This guy is the best."

"Here's your latte." Eve handed a cup to Jordyn.

Nick approached. "Drone is ready to go."

"Good. Let's send it up to get the imaging." Jordyn sipped her coffee.

Nick jogged back to the van.

"Eve, I've drawn some maps, taken notes and pictures. You can transcribe them back at the lab. Set up the survey equipment. We'll use the points of interest to create a digital map." Jordyn bit her lip. "I know, a bit out of order than our usual, but this scene is anything but usual with the upcoming hurricane and a shooter wanting to shut us down."

Colt inched forward. "Bones, myself and the constabulary are here to protect you all."

Eve squatted beside the K-9. "He's very handsome. How did he get his name?"

"When he was a puppy, he grabbed a turkey leg bone and tried to run away with it." Colt brought out a treat shaped like a bone from his belt pouch and tossed it to his dog. "I named him appropriately."

Bones gulped the treat down in one bite.

A commotion on the property's edge drew Colt's attention. The female reporter had ducked around the caution tape, out of Constable Greer's reach. The woman darted toward Jordyn with a cameraman scurrying behind her.

Colt's hand flew to his sidearm. "Bones, guard!"

The K-9 leaped to his feet, barking and baring his teeth.

The reporter stopped. "Whoa, now. I'm not here to hurt anyone. I just want to talk to the premier's daughter." She raised her microphone. "You are Dr. Jordyn Miller, right?"

Colt extended his hand. "Please give me your identification, Miss—"

"Baine. Ursula Baine. Charock Channel 5 News." She withdrew her wallet and passed Colt her driver's license. She gestured toward the cameraman. "This is Freddy."

Colt reviewed the picture and then the blond in front of him. "You just trespassed over a police-issued line."

"So this is a crime scene?" She stuck the microphone in Colt's face.

He noted the red blinking light on the camera. "I can't comment on an ongoing investigation. Now, I'm gonna have to ask you to leave."

Bones growled, reacting to the tone of Colt's voice.

Jordyn placed her hand on Colt's arm. "It's okay, Colt. Let me handle this." She turned to Ursula. "Yes, I'm Dr. Jordyn Miller, forensic anthropologist."

"And the premier's daughter?"

"Correct."

Ursula turned to Freddy. "You getting this?"

He nodded.

"Why are you here, Dr. Miller? Did you find remains?"

Jordyn chuckled. "Well, we *are* next to a cemetery. The only comment I can make is, we're investigating and will know more soon. Now, if you'll excuse us, my team has work to do."

"But—"

Colt placed his hand over her microphone. "That's all. Please leave the property."

Bones growled once more.

Ursula's eyes widened. She nodded and retreated under the tape with her cameraman but remained on-site.

Another police cruiser arrived at the scene.

Jordyn crossed her arms. "More police? Don't we have enough?"

"You can thank your father. He just told me—"

"Wait, you spoke with my father again?" Her voice held irritation.

"He's pressuring me, Jordyn."

"Well, don't let him. I can't work with all these people. Please keep them out of my investigation." She waved at her team and gestured for the crime scene unit to follow her.

Colt pointed after the woman his K-9 was there to protect. "Bones, heel."

He bit down hard on the inside of his mouth, frustration setting in. *Great.*

The premier was breathing down Colt's neck to protect his daughter—but that same daughter didn't even want him around.

How could he keep her safe if she wouldn't let him?

THREE

Colt surveyed the scene hours later as the ground-penetrating radar found additional unmarked graves. Jordyn's drone had also imaged the area. The constable assigned to Morgan had confirmed he'd safely dropped her off at work but remained parked on the street to keep watch. Colt had given Jordyn this update but kept his distance, ensuring Bones guarded his ex-girlfriend. Colt had to let her do her job, and he couldn't do that by hovering, especially when he sensed she didn't want him there. Not that he blamed her. He had broken her heart—and his.

When he'd discovered how much she loved children and wanted a large family, he knew he had to end things. He had vowed not to have kids because the thought of passing down his dyslexia to a child plagued him. Colt had struggled with the learning disability and the bullying from his schoolmates. He could not put a child through that agony. Once he'd been diagnosed,

Colt's reading slowly improved. However, he still struggled with self-confidence, even after asking God to eliminate his feelings of inadequacy.

And then there was his brother. Colt didn't feel worthy of love because he had failed Linc. How could someone love a man who had caused his own brother's death? For both those reasons, he'd ended his relationship with Jordyn.

"We found another one!"

Nick's cry shifted Colt back to the crime scene. He straightened. That now made five graves.

Not good. Lord, is one of these Linc? Guilt locked Colt's muscles like stretched elastic bands, ready to snap at any moment. He raked his fingers through his hair and returned to where Jordyn stood. "What are we looking at here, Jordyn? Do you suspect foul play?"

Her lips briefly flattened into a rigid line. "Or a family plot."

"I don't buy that. Why would a family bury their own in unmarked graves? It doesn't make sense."

Bones shifted position at the sound of Colt's voice.

"Stay. Good boy." Colt turned his gaze back to Jordyn.

She shrugged. "Well, Eve and Nick have finished taking pictures of a couple graves, and the rest of the team is working hard to finish. Hopefully, we'll know more soon."

Raindrops splattered around them.

"Great. The storm is coming. We need more time. It's too large of a site to finish today." Jordyn walked over to the newest grave and squatted.

Colt studied the sky. The dark clouds threatened to open up at any moment. *Lord, help Jordyn's team finish quickly and get the remains transported.*

"Colt! We got something." Constable Greer rushed toward him, raising her tablet.

Colt checked to make sure another constable was staying close to Jordyn before running and meeting Greer halfway, near the growing crowd of onlookers. "What is it?"

Greer tapped the device. "The judge came through. We got the video footage. I checked this morning's, but nothing to report. Just us coming on the scene."

Good for you, Premier Miller. "Let me see it. Go back to around nine last night. The tip was called in after 1:00 a.m."

Greer adjusted the video line to the appropriate time and tapped on the arrow to play.

Darkness greeted them, along with a glow from the spotlight on the warehouse property. The camera's angle gave them a perfect view of the makeshift graveyard. A deer walked across the lawn and stopped by a balsam fir, nibbling on the grass.

"Fast-forward." Colt peered closer at the screen, not wanting to miss anything.

Greer dragged the progress bar farther down the line.

An image passed by in the frame.

Colt pointed to the screen. "Stop there. Rewind."

She obeyed and once again hit Play.

A hooded figure walked across the grounds and toward the tree, holding a backpack.

High-pitched growls sounded in the distance, and the figure retreated to the tree line. Moments later, two lynxes skulked back and forth over the property. They stopped, baring their teeth before swatting their paws at each other as if staking their claim.

The animals brought the carvings back to Colt's mind. He would ask Jordyn if she found more in the other graves. "Fast-forward again."

Greer advanced the progress bar until another figure appeared. She stopped and hit Play.

A security guard walked to the edge of the warehouse property, shining a flashlight toward the cemetery. A few seconds later, another figure dashed behind him, a ponytail bouncing under their hat.

"Wait, was that a woman?" Greer asked, freezing the frame and leaning closer. "Sure looks like it." She pressed Play again.

The footage revealed the guard turning and

walking back out of the camera's view. Colt and Greer reviewed the rest of the video, but no other suspicious movement had been captured.

Could the gravedigger have been a woman? "We need to find that security guard. I'm guessing he's probably off shift by now. Can you look into it?" Colt asked.

"On it." Greer scurried toward the building's entrance.

"Constable, can you tell us what's going on?" An onlooker waved her hand at Colt. "It looks like you're digging up skeletons. Is that true?"

Light rain showered the area as the caution tape flapped in the breeze. Soon the rain storm would be upon them.

He walked over to the group. "No comment. Folks, time to leave. They're predicting Hurricane Jezebel will be fierce. This rain is only the beginning. Gather provisions and take shelter."

"But we want to know what's going on!" another person yelled.

Colt noted that a constable was standing near the news van. He motioned to him. "Can you move this crowd back?"

"I'll take care of it." The man raced over to another constable, and together they relocated the onlookers to the warehouse property.

"Colt!" Jordyn yelled a few hours later. She ran toward him with Bones at her side. "I have news."

The twisted expression on her face told Colt it

wasn't good. He balled his hands into fists, bracing himself. "What is it?"

"Well, I can't say for certain until we examine the skeletons closer, but..." She hesitated.

Was she trying to prepare him? "Just tell me."

"We have a killer on our hands. Two skeletons have markings consistent with some sort of trauma."

Lightning flashed beyond the tree line, followed by a thunderclap, as if emphasizing Jordyn's findings.

Just what they needed. Storms and a potential killer on the loose. Would the normally quiet town of Charock Harbour survive news of this magnitude?

"Wait, did you say killer? A serial killer?" Ursula Baine asked from behind them.

Colt turned.

She shoved the microphone in Colt's face once again. The camera's red light popped on. They were filming.

"You heard it, folks—we have a serial killer among us, and he's burying bones right here in this makeshift graveyard." She moved in front of a mound of soil. "Let's call him the BoneDigger. Dr. Jordyn Miller is on the case."

Colt stepped into her personal space. "We didn't say that." Heat flushed through his body, but he pushed his anger inward. "You need to turn that camera off and leave, Ms. Baine, or I will have you arrested for hampering an investigation. Do you understand?"

Beside him, Bones let out a low warning growl.

Ursula put up her hand. "I'm going. But mark my words. We will get this story—with or without your help." She grasped her cameraman's arm. "Let's go." They stomped back to their van.

Jordyn gently grabbed Colt's arm. "There's more."

He froze. Something in her voice told him what she was about to say would be personal. "What?"

"My team is still examining, but I found this in the last grave." She lifted a bagged object and handed it to him. "There's an inscription on it. I'm so sorry."

A college ring.

Colt's matching ring weighed heavily on his own finger. *Lord, no.*

Dread turned his stomach to lead. He read the inscription on the band: *We love you, Linc.*

A possible serial killer had murdered his brother.

And it was all Colt's fault.

Raindrops fell onto Jordyn's protective suit, but she didn't care. The remorse on Colt's face struck her to the core. The man needed her right now, and even though he'd broken her heart, she couldn't abandon him. She recognized the guilt that traveled through his veins. He had often talked about the fight he'd had with Lincoln that day, a stupid argument over a girl they'd both liked. Colt had told Lincoln how he felt about her, but later found his brother kissing her in the college library, claiming she came on to him. That was the same day Colt had left Lincoln on the side of the road.

Jordyn's thoughts turned to her sister's betrayal, but her situation was different. Morgan had purposely set out to steal Jordyn's fiancé. For some odd reason, her sister had been jealous of Jordyn's accomplishments, so she'd lured Tyler into a secret relationship but had supposedly fallen in love with the man. She'd finally admitted the truth just as Jordyn was about to take her first step down the church aisle to marry Tyler. It was a day Jordyn had tried to erase from her memory.

Morgan and Tyler were now married with two kids. Jordyn adored Ginny and Pepper but didn't get to see them often. She longed to restore her relationship with Morgan, but the betrayal still went too deep.

Another flash of lightning jolted her to the present and the frozen state of the man before her. She brought him into her arms.

He clung to her tight.

Bones whimpered at their feet, sensing his handler's distress.

Jordyn tightened her embrace as memories of

their good times together enveloped her, flooding her with emotions she'd struggled to keep at bay since she first saw him a few hours ago. "I'm sorry, Colt. Perhaps someone stole Lincoln's ring and those remains aren't his."

Colt stepped back, breaking their hold. "How can you say that after what you know?"

"Anything's possible. Once I get the bones back to the lab and finish our findings, we'll get our medical examiner to request the dental records." Jordyn looked at the five graves as the rain began to fall harder. "We need to move faster."

"Wait, did you find anything besides the ring?" Colt asked.

"No. Like what?"

"Linc always wore a chain with a guitar pendant. Mom had it specifically designed for him. He loved writing songs and played his guitar every day." Colt fixed his eyes on the ring. "I think not hearing him play has been hardest on her."

Remorse lodged a knot in Jordyn's throat, and she swallowed. "Do you want to call her?"

He snapped his gaze to hers. "Not until we find out for sure it's him. I can't do that to her. She already doesn't speak to me. If we're wrong...well, I'm not sure how she'd react."

"Understood. How's your dad?"

"Still leading his firefighters with a heavy hand."

Jordyn remembered Chief Dennis Peters as being a drillmaster, but even though he'd sometimes been hard on his team, they still loved him.

Colt gazed at his brother's last resting site. "Can I see Linc before you finish?"

"Of course, but don't touch anything." She walked over to the grave and crouched. Bones sat nearby but not close enough to contaminate the scene. *Smart dog.*

Colt surveyed the bones lying in the dirt and blew out a ragged breath as a mournful expression haunted his face.

"I'll give you a moment." She stood and walked over to Eve. "I believe this may have been his brother, so give him a few minutes. Then bag and label each bone." She paused. "And do another check in the grave. Colt feels his brother would have been wearing a chain. I want to find it so he can have full closure." It was the least she could do to help ease the man's pain and guilt.

Eve nodded. "It's gonna be a long day."

No kidding.

Later that afternoon, Jordyn walked away from the site and dug her phone out of her bag. She dialed her sister's number. Even though they hadn't been on the best terms lately, she still needed her twin to be safe.

"Jordyn, what's up?" Morgan asked.

"Checking in to ensure you're okay."

"I'm fine, no thanks to you."

Jordyn chewed on her lip, biting down on the words she wanted to say. "Morgan, this isn't my fault. If you only knew what we found, you wouldn't say that."

"What is it?"

A few questions rose in Jordyn's mind. Was the killer still active? Had they killed again? If so, would they try to bury the body here?

Jordyn prayed they weren't in danger because of this maniac… Not that she really offered prayers to God much anymore, after all the hurt He'd allowed in her life. "Can't really say—but please take extra precautions. Promise me you'll let the constabulary keep watch over you."

Her sister puffed out air. "I will. Dad would never let me hear the end of it if I dodged my security detail."

Jordyn snickered. "Like you did back in college?"

"You remember that?"

"Of course." She wiped the raindrops from her forehead. "How are Ginny and Pepper?"

"Fine. They're both doing well in school. Ginny loves gymnastics, and Pepper is learning how to play the flute. But you would know if you came around more often." She harrumphed. "I need fresh air."

"Colt said to stay inside, Morgan." Would her twin listen? "And it's not that simple." How could she get her sister to realize seeing them together as a family hurt?

"What? You're still angry with me and Tyler?" A slamming door sounded through the phone, followed by a roar of traffic. "Grow up and get over it, Jordyn. Maybe you should date someone."

Jordyn glanced at Colt, who was leaning over one of the graves.

Truth be told, she'd never wanted to date again after the man before her had crushed her heart. She'd fallen quickly and deeply for Colt Peters. No, failed love was too hard to come back from. Twice. *I can't do that again.*

A commotion sounded in her ear, followed by her sister's scream.

"Morgan! What's happening?"

Bones barked, circling her legs.

Jordyn's cry drew Colt's attention, and he bounded over to her.

"Sissy, help—"

The call dropped.

Fear skittered over her skin, sending chills to her spine. "Morgan!"

Something had happened. Morgan hadn't called her *Sissy* since Jordyn's would-be wedding day.

Nausea thickened Jordyn's throat, and she latched on to Colt's arm. "Morgan's in trouble. We need to get over there."

Colt's cell phone chimed, and he looked at his screen. His jaw dropped.

"What is it?" Jordyn asked, holding her breath. *I can't take anymore, Lord. Where are You?*

Colt turned the screen toward her.

A picture of Morgan, unconscious, in the back of a truck, with a text below it that said:

You can't save her. Dr. Jordyn Miller will pay for interfering.

"No!" Jordyn gasped as a thought surfaced. "He thinks he has me. He's abducted the wrong twin! I have to get to her." She hurried toward her vehicle.

Bones barked.

"Jordyn, stop!" Colt yelled.

Bones tugged on Jordyn's PPE suit, pulling her backward and stopping her from advancing any farther.

She turned to the dog just as an explosion rocked the area, sending pieces of the forensic van into the air. Jordyn's hands clenched into fists as realization iced her veins.

Bones had saved her life this time. But someone wanted to stop their investigation.

FOUR

Wind whipped around the cemetery parking lot as Colt positioned himself in front of Jordyn with Bones at his side, shielding her from further harm. She had wanted to stay on-site while the firefighters extinguished the forensics van so she could see if the bones her team had collected were still intact. Doubt swam in Colt's mind. *Lord, help Dad's crew save them. Those victims need to be identified so their families can have peace.* Constables had escorted Ursula's team off the property, but Colt guessed that wouldn't be the last time they would hear from the relentless reporter. Not that he blamed her. She only wanted to report the happenings of Charock Harbour's community.

The rain had intensified. Colt had to get everyone inside. Fast. He observed the smoke rising from the van. At least the rain had helped put out the fire. Maybe in time to preserve the remains.

"How much longer will they be?" Jordyn bit

her nails. "Dr. Jones will reprimand me for leaving the scene, but I want to go talk to my sister's coworkers. Perhaps someone witnessed something that might help us find her. Eve and Nick can continue here, along with the rest of the team."

Bones whined and circled the duo protectively.

"You're not an investigator. I know how much you enjoy solving mysteries like Nancy Drew, but going there isn't wise, Jordyn. We need to keep you concealed. Besides, Constable Michaels is on-site now, interviewing people. Let them do their job." Colt reached into his pouch and tossed Bones a treat, then fastened the leash onto the dog's collar.

Colt's father approached and adjusted his chief's helmet as he nodded. "Hey, son. Jordyn. How are you?"

"Could be better, but it's nice to see you again, Dennis." Jordyn shifted her stance. "Please tell me we didn't lose everything in the fire."

"Thankfully, the rain helped put the flames out fast. You can go check it out now. Just be—"

Jordyn hurried toward the van, not waiting for the rest of his father's sentence.

"Jordyn! Wait for us." Colt unleashed his German shepherd. "Bones, guard."

The dog ran after his subject.

Fire Chief Dennis Peters clucked his tongue. "I see she hasn't changed. Still impatient."

"Yes, and stubborn. Thanks for getting here so quickly, Dad." Colt hesitated. Should he tell his father they'd found Linc's ring? No, not yet.

"Happy to help. How are you doing?"

"Fine." Colt kept his eye on Jordyn and Bones.

"I miss our talks. Our Sunday lunches after church just aren't the same without you and—" He stopped. An awkward silence continued before his father spoke again. "She won't say it, but your mom misses you, too, Colt."

Colt turned his focus back to his father. The man's forlorn expression tugged at Colt's heart as a question surfaced. How would Colt ever bridge the breach with his mother? It was his deepest longing, but the hole had only grown over the years since his brother's disappearance—and now, how could he tell his mother Linc had possibly been murdered by a serial killer? She'd never forgive Colt.

"I'll bring Bones by soon for another visit." Colt squashed the emotions threatening to bring tears and averted his eyes back to Jordyn. She was leaning farther into the van's rear entrance—or what was left of it. "Mom still holds me accountable for Linc not coming home that day, Dad. She refuses to talk to me, even after ten years. What can I do to change that? Nothing I've tried has worked. I'm all out of ideas." He flattened his lips into an impregnable line. Why would a mother ignore her only living son?

His father's radio squawked, requesting his presence back at their station. He responded to Dispatch before squeezing Colt's shoulder. "Son, I gotta go, but listen to me—forgive yourself first. I know you're feeling guilty about Linc. It's time to put the darkness behind us. Until light shines again, we'll never move on and be a family. Think about that." His father hustled to his Suburban and hopped inside. His tires squealed as he pulled out of the parking lot.

God, is Dad right? Show me how to forgive myself. Colt wanted nothing more than to feel his mother's love and respect again.

Even if he himself didn't believe he deserved it after failing his brother.

I'm so sorry, Linc.

Questions haunted his mind. What had happened that night after Colt had driven away, leaving Linc behind? Who had killed him, and why?

"No!"

Jordyn's cry lurched him back to the situation, and he hurried forward. "What's going on?" Colt put the past in the background, turning his attention to the woman in front of him. "What did you find?"

"Charred remains. Thankfully, only one set of bones was placed in the van, and firefighters saved them before they completely turned to ash, but it will make our examination more challenging."

Colt was aware of her desire to prove her abilities to her father and win his respect, but it was an uphill battle. Russell had wanted her to go into politics, but she'd refused. Her passion was the human body, and anthropology had always intrigued her.

A gust of wind flipped Jordyn's hood off, exposing her brown hair and reminding Colt of the bad weather. Was the hurricane coming earlier than expected? He needed to get her to safety. "Jordyn, I'm sorry, but we have to get you somewhere safe. The storm is approaching quickly."

"I will, but I have to know first how this happened."

"I can answer that." A female firefighter held out a charred object inside an evidence bag. "Found this under the van. Looks like it was set off by a remote detonator."

Constable Lavigne joined the group. "How could the BoneDigger have planted an explosive right under our noses?"

Lavigne had already taken up Ursula's coined name for the suspect. Colt surmised it wouldn't be long before the entire community did the same.

Colt examined the explosive. "Very good question. Maybe someone in the crowd saw something."

"My guess is one of *them* is responsible," Jordyn said. "How else could they have gotten so close?"

"I'll leave you guys to it. Gotta get back to my squad." The firefighter dashed toward her truck.

Colt addressed his fellow officer. "She's right. It's the only answer."

"That person wanted these remains unidentifiable." Jordyn hissed out a breath. "They almost succeeded."

Colt didn't want to ask, but he had to. "Which remains were—"

Jordyn gripped his arm. "Don't worry. His bones haven't been bagged yet."

Colt exhaled. *Thank You, Lord. One small blessing in this mess.*

"And, Colt, I meant to tell you. Eve didn't find a guitar pendant. I'm so sorry."

He nodded, pushing his emotions to the background. Right now, he had a job to do. He passed the evidence bag with the explosive device to Lavigne. "Get this to Forensics and tell us if they find anything else. Also, can you try to trace the text I received on my cell phone? I'm guessing it's probably from a burner, but I want to check."

"On it."

"Who's running point on the witness interrogations?" Colt asked.

"Constable Greer. She's got them over there." Lavigne gestured toward the warehouse.

The female constable was speaking to the crowd at the corner of the building, where she'd gathered them for shelter from the pelting rain and rising winds. The newer constable had proved her worth over the past few weeks, and her surprising street smarts had impressed their sergeant. "Good. Did you find the security guard?"

"Gave that task to Greer too. I asked her to contact you." Lavigne raised the bag. "Gotta run. Good to meet you, Dr. Miller." The constable darted over to his vehicle.

Colt peered inside the back of the van. "Wow. Whoever did this knew what they were doing."

"Makes me so angry. How could they have been this prepared, though? Did they know I'd been called to the scene—and if so, how?"

"All good questions. But for now, we need—"

"Constable Peters, report." Sergeant Warren's voice boomed through Colt's radio.

Colt flinched at his leader's commanding tone. *Not good.* "Peters here."

"Need you down at the courthouse. Stat."

Jordyn's eyes widened, fear visibly contorting her pretty face. "That's where Morgan works. What did they find?"

"What's going on, Sergeant?" Colt asked.

"Eyewitness is requesting Dr. Miller's presence. Said she'll only speak to her. Not sure why. I have the premier breathing down my neck, Peters. We need to find his other daughter and also keep Dr. Miller safe." He paused. "After you're finished at the courthouse, take the premier's daughter somewhere secure."

Colt clicked on his radio to respond. "Understood. On it." He turned to Jordyn. "Let's go."

She nodded. "But first, let me send the team home. We'll come back first thing in the morning. There's still lots to do here. Police will need to keep the scene secure for us."

"I'll get Sergeant Warren on it."

She jogged toward Eve, Nick and the others.

"Bones, heel." Colt followed with one thought on his mind…

Keeping Jordyn safe from not only a possible serial killer but now an impending hurricane could prove deadly. They were running out of time.

Jordyn ducked and held the hood of her raincoat firmly in place as she hustled up the courthouse steps. The rain continued to hammer the region, along with rising wind gusts. Was it a preamble of what was to come? Forecasters had predicted the hurricane to hit within a few days. That gave Jordyn time to talk to the eyewitness who had requested her presence and finish their examination of the scene. Colt and Bones flanked her as they entered the building. Two constables stationed across the street kept an eye out for any suspicious activity. Her father had ordered Jordyn not to go anywhere without protection. With one daughter missing and the other in danger, Premier Russell Miller wasn't about to take any further risks. He had assured Jordyn he had the deputy superintendent pulling out all the stops to protect his family. Jordyn pitied any constables who impeded his orders.

She noted the empty lobby. Normally, the courthouse was flooded with activity, but many had retreated in anticipation of Jezebel's path. Some had also fled the area, taking shelter in other parts of the province not expected to be badly hit. *If only I could do the same.* However, Jordyn had a job to do. Examine those bones and find her sister. Morgan's scream still rang in Jordyn's ears, along with her words:

Your job puts your family in jeopardy.

Morgan's last call for help bounced around Jordyn's head like a tennis ball in a heated match. Was her sister in the BoneDigger's hands? Ginny and Pepper needed their mother back, and Jordyn would do anything for her nieces—even if she wasn't in their lives right now. Jordyn wanted to change their relationship.

She also wanted the bond she'd once had with Morgie—the nickname Jordyn had given her sister when they were five. But would Jordyn ever be able to put the hurt behind her? Its darkness still held her captive. She knew bitterness had taken over, and it was time to let go. Jordyn's life needed a ray of sunshine. Dealing with remains and death all day long can get to a person after a while. Not that she didn't enjoy her job, as it entailed more than examining bones—but when she stumbled upon victims who had died from sinister causes, it disturbed her to see the evil in the world. *God, how can You allow the darkness?*

The question plagued her daily.

She inhaled deeply and approached the security desk with Colt and Bones by her side.

The balding guard straightened in his chair. "Can I help you?"

Colt raised his credentials. "Constable Colt Peters, and this is Dr. Jordyn Miller. We're here to join Constable Michaels. Can you direct us to that floor?"

"Right, your sergeant called. Third floor, second meeting room on the right." The older guard gestured to the left. "Elevators are around the corner."

Colt tapped the counter. "Thanks." He turned to Jordyn and gently pulled on Bones's leash. "Let's go."

They proceeded around the corridor, and Colt punched the up button.

They entered the elevator, and Colt hit the button for the third floor. The car jolted upward.

"Colt, where was Michaels when Morgan was kidnapped? Wasn't he supposed to be in a cruiser protecting her?" Jordyn failed to keep the sharpness out of her tone, but she required answers.

Bones nudged himself closer to her, obviously in response to her curt tone.

"I'll be sure to ask him later."

She exhaled. "I'm sorry. This isn't your fault, Colt. I just feel responsible. Someone took my sister, thinking it was me." She sighed. "Morgan's right. I have put my family at risk."

"Hardly, Jordyn. There's no way you're responsible. For all we know, Morgan's abduction may not even be related to your finding the bones."

She tilted her head. "How can you say that after the text you received? They said I had to pay for interfering. It *is* my fault."

He turned to face her and placed his hands on each of her arms, capturing her gaze. "Listen to me. You're only doing your job. Morgan had no right to say that to you. Let's see what this witness has to say, okay?"

She nodded and averted her eyes. Staring at him only brought back emotions she wanted to remain hidden. How could she be around him and still keep that from happening?

Seconds later, the doors opened, and they stepped onto the third floor.

A constable stood in the hallway with his arms crossed. "Good. You're finally here, Peters." He pointed to a door. "This way."

"Got here as quickly as possible," Colt said.

Jordyn smiled. "Good to see you again, Constable Michaels. Can you tell me why this witness asked for me?"

"She wouldn't say but insisted on it. Maybe

she knows you're the premier's daughter and is looking for a reward? You know how some people can be around influential people." Constable Michaels walked up to the door and turned the knob. "Her name is Wanda Harrelson."

Jordyn entered the small office and saw a woman sitting at the table.

The fortysomething woman wore a colorful headband, which held her wiry brown curls in place. She snapped her gum before looking up at them, drumming her hot pink nails on the table. "'Bout time you came."

"She's all yours," Constable Michaels whispered as he backed out of the office and closed the door.

That didn't sound promising. Jordyn looked at Colt and arched her brow in a silent question.

Colt responded with a slight smile before turning to Bones. "Sit." The K-9 obeyed. "I'm Constable Peters. Mrs. Harrelson, can you tell us why you requested Dr. Miller?" Colt sat opposite the woman.

Jordyn leaned against the wall and waited for Wanda's answer.

"It's *Miss*, Constable." She chewed on her gum, popping bubbles. Her eyes rested on Jordyn. "You're the premier's other daughter. The smart one."

Jordyn shoved off from the wall. "How dare you—"

Colt grabbed Jordyn's arm gently. "Miss Harrelson, no need to be rude. Tell us what information you have regarding Morgan Crandall's abduction."

The woman picked at her cuticles. "I want something in return for assisting y'all. I know your father is well-off."

Why did everything come back to her father?

Colt leaned forward. "You tell us what information you have, and we'll go from there. Understood?"

Thankful for Colt's protective presence, Jordyn walked over to the small window. The storm clouds made it look later than it really was outside. When would the darkness dissipate? She brushed off the question and turned back to the woman. "Do you also work with my sister as a court clerk?"

"If you want to call what your sister does here work, then yes."

Jordyn looked at Colt, then Wanda. "What does that mean?"

"She gets away with everything. We do all the work, but she gets the credit. The boss is sweet on her because she's the premier's daughter." She drummed her fingernails once again, the annoying clicking sound booming in the tiny room.

Jordyn balled her hands into fists, curtailing the rising anger. Somehow, she guessed the woman was exaggerating. "Miss Harrelson, please tell us why you called me here. What do you know about Morgan's abduction?"

"What will you give me?"

Colt bolted upright, placed his palms on the table and got in the woman's face. "You can take that up with my boss. Tell us what you know. Now!"

Bones moved closer to Wanda and growled.

The smirk disappeared from Wanda's face, and she recoiled from the angered German shepherd. "Okay, okay. Don't let him bite me."

"Don't give him a reason to." Colt waved his hand at Bones. The dog retreated at Colt's silent command.

Jordyn covered her mouth to hide the chuckle surfacing. She knew Bones wouldn't bite unless ordered to, and she loved how easily the pair worked together. They were a force no one dared to cross.

"I was out having a smoke in the designated area at the side of the building when I heard a scream. A woman in a hat pushed someone into a white truck."

Colt glanced at Jordyn.

She could almost read his thoughts. Was it the same truck that had been following Morgan that morning? "What happened next?"

"She spoke on her cell phone, saying the premier's daughter has been taken care of and now their secret would remain hidden." Wanda blew out another bubble and popped it. "Not sure what that meant. She also called the person her 'love,' so I assumed she was talking to her boyfriend."

Jordyn drew in a sharp breath. "Why didn't you help Morgan?"

"I froze. I saw a shotgun in the truck, and I'm petrified of guns."

"Can you describe the woman?" Colt asked.

"She had her hat pulled down, so I only saw her jawline and blond ponytail." The woman stumbled to her feet. "That's all I know. Can I go now?"

"I want you to come to our station. I'm gonna have a forensic artist talk to you. They're good at drawing out details from witnesses." Colt called his leader and made the arrangements.

Five minutes later, Colt, Jordyn, Wanda, Constable Michaels and Bones stepped off the elevator.

The dog suddenly growled and tried to tug Colt along as he lunged toward the entrance. However, his leash held him firmly in place.

Something had the K-9 agitated.

Colt unholstered his weapon and unclipped the leash. The officer obviously trusted his partner. "Bones, guard." He lifted his gun.

Bones stayed close to Jordyn's side.

The group edged around the corner and into the lobby, both constables pointing their sidearms in different directions.

The guard lay on the floor, with a gunshot wound to his chest.

Jordyn froze.

Movement on the mezzanine drew her attention. A bouncing ponytail flashed in her peripheral view seconds before shotgun blasts shattered the glass door and Wanda dropped to the floor.

Terror iced Jordyn's spine. "No!" She fell to her knees and checked for a pulse. Nothing.

Somehow, the BoneDigger had caught wind of the witness and silenced her before she could identify the woman with the ponytail.

FIVE

"How did the BoneDigger know we were here?" Colt grimaced at his use of Ursula's name for the killer. At this point, they hadn't determined if they had a serial killer on their hands or if the suspect who had buried the skeletons was male or female. Wanda had witnessed a female, and Jordyn had stated she'd seen the same woman on the mezzanine before the shots rang out. However, Wanda wouldn't be able to make any type of identification—she'd died at the scene. Thankfully, the guard was still alive and en route to the hospital, but he hadn't seen who had shot him. The color had drained from Jordyn's face the moment she discovered Wanda had passed. Colt had guessed from her terror-stricken expression that this latest death escalated her concern for Morgan. *Lord, keep Jordyn safe and help us to find Morgan before—*

He couldn't finish the prayer. He was aware of the strained relationship between the twins, but he also knew how much Jordyn loved her sister despite the woman's betrayal. That's what made it so hard for her. Even after Colt had broken up with Jordyn, he had continued to pray for her daily, asking God to help her move past her hurt and restore her bond with her sister. Siblings needed each other. He desperately missed Linc and would do anything to have him back in his life.

Colt spun his college ring around his finger, remembering what the BoneDigger had stolen from him—his brother's life. *I will find you and bring you to justice. Whoever you are.*

"No idea," Michaels said. "Perhaps they followed you from the cemetery?"

"Nope, no tails. I took extra time in coming just to ensure I didn't have one." In a sharp tone, he asked, "Michaels, why didn't you see the truck Wanda referred to? Weren't you guarding Morgan?"

Colt didn't miss his fellow officer's expression turn to one of contempt. Colt needed to dial back his frustration. His colleagues had already labeled him as their sergeant's favorite at their constabulary's station, and the premier had chosen Colt to protect Jordyn. That would add fuel to the fire. But Russell trusted Colt and especially Bones. "I'm sorry. I don't mean to accuse you, but it's my job to protect Jordyn."

"I was breaking up a fight out front around that time." He hung his head. "A diversion to cover the abduction, perhaps?"

The man's tone revealed his angst.

Colt understood. He had also made wrong calls during his career. He couldn't fault Michaels. He'd only been doing his job.

"Perhaps. The suspect may have more helping him." Colt paused. "Or her."

"True. Stay safe."

"You too." Colt zigzagged around the other constables investigating the scene and approached Jordyn.

Bones stood at attention, guarding his subject.

Colt ruffled his partner's ears. "Good job, bud. Jordyn, we'll leave using the rear entrance. Constables are patrolling the area, but I doubt the shooter is still in the vicinity. However, I need to ensure your safety." He clipped his dog's leash back into place.

"I understand. Any updates on the guard's condition?" Jordyn's shaky hand pushed her bag's strap farther up her shoulder.

Her body language failed to suppress her anxiety over not only her sister's abduction but also safety for her own life. Colt knew her well from their relationship and could read her fear even when she tried to hide it.

"They reached the hospital and rushed him into surgery." He nudged her toward the rear exit. "Time to get you somewhere more secure for the night."

She snagged his arm. "Where? This person seems to know everything about me. I don't think I'll be safe at home."

He took her hand, still resting on his arm, and interlocked his fingers in hers. "I hate to say it, but I think your parents' cottage residence would be best. Your dad has added security."

Her face scrunched like a child about to throw a temper tantrum. "My father is the last person I want to be around right now. Isn't there some other place I could hide?"

"Not on such short notice." He hesitated. "I won't take no for an answer. You can be stubborn, but your safety is at risk."

She tilted her head. "Are you implying I have a hard time submitting to authority?"

He didn't miss her joking tone, even in their precarious situation. She always knew how to lighten the mood. He missed their friendship and fun banter.

"Not at all. Just want to keep you safe."

"Well, let me grab some things first." She poked him in the chest. "Since you're in constant contact with Dad, you can call him and make the arrangements. You're staying with us."

Colt bristled. His weary muscles wanted to sink into his own bed, but he set aside his needs.

All he cared about was keeping Jordyn safe from a killer.

Jordyn rubbed her arms. They'd spent the last two days in the damp weather, processing the unmarked graveyard, and she only wanted to settle back at the lab to begin her meticulous inspection of the bones. Her team labored hard to finish at the scene to prepare for their documentation. They would work with Dr. Vance Chambers. Terror bull-rushed Jordyn as questions thundered through her mind. To whom did these bones belong? How had these people died? Her initial assessments had revealed it wasn't from natural causes. *I'm tired of the evil You allow. Why, Lord, why? When will it stop? It's so hard to see You in the darkness.* Jordyn had helped solve many cold cases alongside law enforcement and medical examiners on the Rock. These deaths had been haunting her dreams lately, plunging her mood into the shadows—where she hated to be. Had God abandoned His people? She no longer felt His presence.

Plus, her sister was still missing. Police had failed to find Morgan.

Where are You, God?

"Jordyn, did you hear me?" Colt asked.

His voice and the K-9's bark jolted her to the present, and she blinked to bring the scene before her into view.

Even the German shepherd seemed to sense her mood.

Get a grip. Jordyn swallowed to give herself time to find her voice. "I'm sorry—what did you say?"

"I was just asking if you're almost done at the

scene." Colt pointed. "Looks like the rest of the bones have been bagged."

Jordyn turned her gaze back to the unmarked graves and spotted her team working with the CSI unit. "Yes, we're wrapping up now. Has Sergeant Warren received any more leads on Morgan's—" Hair prickled at the back of Jordyn's neck as a recollection slammed into her mind. "Wait, I just remembered something."

"What?"

She wiped her forehead with the back of her hand. "Didn't Wanda say the suspicious woman called the person she was talking to her 'love'?"

"She did." He snapped his fingers. "We have male and female suspects. Lovers. Two killers?"

"It makes sense. How could whoever kidnapped my sister the other day be in two places at once?"

"They couldn't. That reminds me—Constable Greer hasn't heard from the owner of Charock Lighting. We need to talk to them." He hit the talk button on his radio. "Greer, can you contact Charock Lighting again and tell them if they don't reply today, they'll be hearing from the premier himself? They've been dodging our calls too long." Colt's eyes met hers and he winked.

Jordyn hated when people pulled the premier card, but in this case, it was necessary. They needed answers, and the lighting company's employees may have seen something that could help.

Sara's voice sailed through the radio. "Let me follow up. I'll get back to you."

Jordyn pulled a pair of gloves out of her jacket pocket. "I want to check in with Eve, Nick and the others to see how their documentation is coming."

"Good plan." Colt followed her.

Five hours later, after determining Greta had found all the graves and no other remains appeared on the ground-penetrating radar, Jordyn addressed her team. "Good work, guys. I know with the approaching hurricane and constant criminal threats, you've worked quicker than normal." She turned to Colt. "I can't believe we found five remains."

"Do you suspect foul play?" Colt asked.

"You know that's not for me to determine, but..." She bit her lip.

Colt finished her sentence. "You suspect it."

"I hate to speculate." However, her gut was screaming that these crudely dug graves meant something sinister. "We need to determine what these lynx carvings mean. They were placed in each of their hands for a reason." She gestured toward Constable Lavigne. "CSI is ready to transport the bones to the autopsy lab. Eve, Nick—you good to go?"

"I don't like that we hurried," Nick said. "That's how mistakes happen, and something tells me this case will prove to be a difficult one."

"Agreed." Jordyn checked the time. "Where

did today go? It's nearly dinner, and we haven't eaten. How about I order pizza and have it delivered to the lab?" Dusk would soon be upon them. She shivered from the dampness and studied the cloudy sky, wondering when Jezebel would hit. Hopefully not until they were safe and sound, hunkered down in the lab.

"Yes!" Eve and Nick yelled.

Their cell phones screeched, simultaneously announcing an alert.

Jordyn reached for her phone and read the screen.

Hurricane imminent. Take shelter.

Good thing they had finished at the scene. She scanned the site. *Did we get everything?*

If not, the storm would eliminate all hopes of any other possible evidence.

Colt noted the panic-stricken expressions pass over Jordyn's and her team member's faces. Jezebel's path wouldn't leave the area for hours. "Jordyn, we have to get to safety." But a question lingered in Colt's mind…

Why hadn't Bones alerted to the threat? Even hours before nasty weather hit, his K-9 usually became antsy. He was Colt's personal meteorologist. Bones hated storms.

That fact needled at Colt, and he placed his

hand on his Sig. "Jordyn, something's bothering me."

She finished adding a bone to a paper bag and labeled it before handing it off to the constabulary's forensic unit. She turned. "What?"

"You know how Bones hates storms and knows hours before when it's gonna hit?"

She stiffened. "And he didn't this time."

"Right. Something's wrong." Colt spoke into his radio. "Greer, report."

Seconds later, the radio crackled. "I'm here. What's up?"

"Did you get a weather alert on your cell phone?"

"Yes, why?"

Relief relaxed Colt's shoulders. He was being paranoid. "Nothing." He turned his focus toward the spotlight in the warehouse parking lot. "Did you get in touch with anyone from Charock Lighting?"

"Just finished chatting with the owner. He's given us free reign over his staff. Night security guard is coming on duty."

"Okay, hold him there. I want to talk to him."

"Copy that."

Jordyn opened another bag. "So we're good? The alert is real?"

"Sounds like it."

"Shouldn't we leave then?"

"I just need a few minutes with the guard."

Colt ruffled Bones's ears. "Why aren't you nervous, bud?"

Bones barked and moved closer to Colt.

The team finished and disassembled their equipment. The forensic unit loaded the bones into the replacement van and would deliver all the evidence to Autopsy at the Health Sciences Centre, where Jordyn's lab was located next to the university. Eve and Nick had left in their vehicle.

The wind had strengthened but was still not at hurricane force. Had the storm stalled, or had the alert been a false alarm? Either way, Colt wanted to get Jordyn to safety. "You ready to go?"

She dug out her cell phone. "I'll place my pizza order on the way to the lab."

"First, we need to head to the warehouse and talk to the night watchman. He may have seen something the other night." Colt reattached Bones's leash.

The trio headed toward the steel door at the northeast corner of the building. Colt yanked it open. "After you."

They entered the darkened, silent hallway.

Colt pressed his radio button. "Greer, we're here. Where are you?"

"Guard station," she responded. "Second door around the corner."

Moments later, the three entered the small but state-of-the-art security room. Monitors lined the walls, and a guard sat in front of multiple computers.

Sara Greer turned from the window. "Peters, this is the night watchman, Kalvin Anderson. Kalvin, Constable Colt Peters and his K-9, Bones."

Colt stuck out his hand. "Good to meet you. This is forensic anthropologist Dr. Jordyn Miller."

The forty-ish man pushed himself up and grasped the offered hand with a firm grip, his frame towering over Colt. "Nice to meet you." He turned to Jordyn, holding out his hand. "Ah, the premier's daughter."

"Yes."

Kalvin inched closer to Jordyn. "Heard lots about you."

Bones growled.

Colt squared his shoulders. "Sir, can you back up? Bones is tasked to protect Dr. Miller. He doesn't like that you're so close."

The man raised his hands in a yielding gesture and returned to his desk. "So sorry. I have a habit of doing that around pretty women."

Colt eyed the man's wedding ring, bothered by his flirty attitude. "I bet your wife doesn't like that habit."

"Nah. I'm harmless and she knows it." Kalvin dropped into his chair. "What can I do for ya, Constable Peters?"

Colt unsnapped his jacket pocket and retrieved

his pen and notebook. "Do you work only the evening shifts?"

"Yup. I'm here every night. Heard you had some strange happenings. What's going on?"

Greer tapped the window. "We can't talk about an ongoing investigation, but you have a perfect view of the Charock Cemetery from here."

"I do, and it creeps me out." The man drummed his fingers on the desk.

Just a habit—or was he nervous?

"Did you see anything suspicious two nights ago?" Colt asked. "We know from the video surveillance you went outside and had a smoke."

Kalvin pushed away from the desk, his expression darkening. "How were you able to see the video?"

He *was* nervous. Why?

"Search warrant from a judge allowed us to look at the footage," Colt said. "Why are you so nervous?"

The man let out an extended sigh. "Because I took an extra break that night, and if my boss finds out, he could sack me. He's too busy to look at the footage, so please don't tell him."

"Well, did you see anything on these extra breaks?" Jordyn asked. "Did you find the bones and call in an anonymous tip?"

"Bones? What bones?" The man's Adam's apple bounced as he swallowed.

The dog growled.

Colt cleared his throat to silence Jordyn and his K-9. "We can't discuss that. Tell us if you saw anything."

"I thought I did at one point, but it was a couple of lynxes prancing around the area. They do that often."

"What about a woman?" Greer moved beside Colt. "I reviewed the video, and it reveals someone with a ponytail walking behind you. You must have seen her."

"I didn't." He grasped the edge of his desk in a viselike grip. "Don't tell my boss. I'm supposed to be guarding this place. I swear, I didn't see a woman." He pushed himself up and tidied his uniform. "Now, if you'll excuse me, I need to get back to work."

Colt studied the man's face. Nothing in his body language revealed deception.

Another dead end.

Colt brought out a business card from his pocket and passed it to Kalvin. "If you think of anything else, please call."

Kalvin nodded.

The group left the security station, leaving the guard alone.

"What's your take on Kalvin?" Greer whispered.

"Definitely a flirt," Jordyn said. "He was jittery about something, though."

Colt gestured for them to move out of the building.

They stepped outside. The rain had returned, with increasing wind gusts.

"I agree with you, Jordyn—but nothing really stood out. He's probably just trying to hide his long breaks. Perhaps he's a slacker and doesn't want his boss to know?" Colt turned to Greer. "Since you're on the late shift, can you follow us to the lab? I want another set of eyes at the perimeter. I don't trust the BoneDigger. He's been too quiet the last couple of days."

"Copy that. Stay safe, you two." Greer hesitated. "Sorry, Bones. I mean, you three." She chuckled and hustled to her cruiser.

Jordyn's cell phone chimed, and she checked her screen. "Eve and Nick arrived at the lab, along with Forensics. They delivered the bones."

"Good. Let's get out of the rain and head there." Colt opened the back door to his car, and Bones hopped inside.

Jordyn jumped into the passenger seat.

Colt's cell phone rang, and he withdrew it as he climbed into the vehicle. He placed it into the holder hooked to his console and caught the name on the screen. "It's your father."

"Great. He's all we need right now." Jordyn rested her head back. "Take it, or he'll keep calling."

Colt started the engine and tapped on Accept. "Good evening, sir."

"Is Jordyn with you?" The premier's tone was harsh.

"I'm here, Dad," Jordyn answered. "We're just leaving the site now."

"You headed here again for the night?" he asked.

"No, I want to hunker down at Autopsy. We have work to do."

Colt drove out of the parking lot. "Sir, the hurricane is supposed to hit at any time now. It's already raining and windy out here."

"That's not what meteorologists are saying. The worst is coming tomorrow afternoon."

What? "Sir, didn't you get the weather alert earlier? It said there was an imminent threat and to take shelter." Colt flicked his signal light on and headed toward the lab.

"What are you talking about?" the premier asked. "I would've been informed about an alert."

Colt jerked his gaze to Jordyn's seconds before Bones barked.

A drone appeared in front of Colt's K-9 vehicle, heading directly at them.

Colt swerved, hit loose gravel and careened toward an oncoming car.

Jordyn screamed.

Colt's earlier concern regarding the alert had been accurate.

Somehow, the BoneDigger had hacked the alert system to get them off the site and sent a drone after them.

Would he take his revenge for uncovering his hidden cemetery plot?

SIX

"Hold on!" Colt tightened his grip on the steering wheel and wrenched the SUV away from the approaching vehicle, barely missing a deadly impact. Colt checked his rearview and side mirrors, searching for the drone. He grimaced. The drone was gearing up for another attack. Could they outrun it? Colt accelerated, and his vehicle lurched forward at high speed. The tires hit a patch of pooled water, and he hydroplaned, swerving toward the median.

Jordyn clutched the console.

Bones barked. He sensed Colt's anxiety. The dog knew him well.

Once again, Colt righted the cruiser and narrowly missed the barrier. *Lord, get me off this highway.* It didn't help that they had a madman's drone on their tail along this dangerous, twisty road. He had to shake whoever was determined to shove them over the side. This highway hugged the ocean, and the deadly drop would not end well. *You've got this. Remember your defensive-driving training.* Colt punched the gas and prayed for the rain to lessen so they'd make it to town quickly.

"Jordyn, what's happening?" The premier's voice boomed through the vehicle's Bluetooth.

Colt had forgotten Jordyn's father was still on the line. "Sir, we're being attacked by an aggressive drone. I gotta call it in, so we need to sign off."

"That highway is dangerous," the premier said. "Please save my daughter! I can't lose another one."

"Dad!" Jordyn yelled. "Colt is an excellent driver. Trust him."

"Call me when you're safe. Love you." He ended the conversation.

Colt contacted Dispatch and asked for assistance, then gave them the details and their location.

The drone sped on ahead of his SUV and pivoted, facing their windshield and revealing what Colt had missed when the aircraft first attacked.

Weaponry hanging from the device.

Colt gasped. The drone was moving in for a clear shot, directly aimed at them. "Cover and hold on!"

The aircraft fired multiple shots just as Colt ducked and jerked the cruiser to the right, diverting them onto the ramp to take them downtown.

The bullets barely missed, peppering the roadway beside them.

Colt needed to lose the drone among the buildings. They had been too out in the open. *Thank You, Lord, for keeping us safe on the highway. Show me where to go.* His condo building in the distance caught his attention. They'd be safe if they could get inside the underground parking garage. Colt checked his mirror. The drone had followed, but the wind and rain had picked up, causing it to sway. *Thank You.* Perhaps the weather would play to their advantage. He knew it would still be able to fly but prayed it would at least slow down slightly so he could try to lose it. Colt took a hard right and turned down a side street close to his condo.

Sirens sounded in the distance. Good. The additional help would hopefully scare whoever was manning the drone from pursuing further.

Colt lowered his window and grabbed his access card from his cruiser's console. He swiped the card, and the parking garage door started to lift.

"Hurry, hurry!" Colt yelled at the door, as if it could understand. He stepped on the gas and drove under the half-open door, praying whoever was flying the contraption had failed to see them enter the garage. He slammed on the brakes and hit the close button before driving down the ramp to the lower level. Seconds later, he parked between two minivans and cut the engine. He turned to Jordyn. "You okay?"

She nodded.

However, the rapid rise and fall of her chest told him otherwise. She was hyperventilating.

"Breathe. In. Out. Long breaths." He reached out and squeezed her shoulder. "You've got this. We're okay."

Colt flipped on the interior light to check on his K-9. "Bones, talk to me."

The German shepherd barked.

"Good, bud." *Thanks for keeping us safe, Lord.*

His leader's voice blared through the cruiser's radio. "Peters, report. Heard you're being attacked by a drone."

"We lost 'em, sir. We're taking cover in my condo's secured parking garage and will head to the university's lab after we wait here for a bit." Colt inhaled deeply to shake off his own jittery nerves.

"Perhaps you should get to the station. It's safer here."

Jordyn leaned her head against her window. "Sergeant Warren, I have to begin my examination of the bones. Families are counting on us, and we need to catch the person responsible before he kills again."

The sergeant puffed out a breath. "Your father called and said you'd be stubborn. He's arranging for extra security and provisions."

Jordyn exhaled. "Not surprised. Sorry he's hounding you, sir."

"Not your fault. Peters, let me know when you arrive at the lab. I've sent—Greer to—area to patrol and keep—" his voice cut out.

"Come again, sir. Didn't catch that."

"Sent Greer to watch for the drone."

"Thanks. Talk later." Colt clicked off the radio and turned to Jordyn. "Your father is harsh toward you because he loves you. You know that, right?"

"I used to, but I'm not so sure anymore."

Colt stilled, rubbing the bridge of his nose. What did that mean? "Why do you say that?"

"Not now. I'm tired and edgy. The last couple of days have been exhausting, and we're not even close to finishing with this case. When can we go?"

"Soon." Colt dropped his line of questioning and eased his head out the window. He listened for the buzzing of an approaching drone.

Silence filled the darkened garage.

"K-9 unit 2bravo8, report your location." Constable Michaels's voice broke the stillness.

"Hiding in an underground parking garage on Fifth Street," Colt said. "Where's the drone?"

"No further sightings. I have other constables searching the area, though. You guys okay?"

He stole a glimpse at Jordyn. Her breathing had regulated. *Good.* He pressed the talk button.

"Just a bit shaken. It's not every day you get fired upon by a weaponized drone."

"True. Had to be someone who's somewhat tech savvy. Drones can be bought and modified easily these days." His grunt filtered through the staticky radio. "Do you have any idea who this could be?"

Colt scratched his forehead. "None. Listen, head to the Health Sciences Centre and secure the area for our arrival. Just so you're aware, the premier is also sending reinforcements."

"Figures. Doesn't he trust us?"

"He's just looking out for his daughter." Colt examined Jordyn's profile. She had closed her eyes, but he guessed she was still listening, choosing to remain silent.

"I get it. His daughters have been targeted. Any father would do the same."

"We'll wait here for a bit. Just to be sure the drone doesn't reappear." Colt wasn't taking any further chances.

"Copy that."

Colt continued to listen for any activity in their vicinity as they waited. For the first time since the early-morning hours, silence covered them in a restful blanket. Colt released a long breath and rested his head against the seat. His thoughts turned to the bones that could be his brother's. Was the BoneDigger responsible? If so, why had he killed Linc? Had his brother come upon something on his walk home? Police had canvassed the area back then and came up with nothing suspicious. *What happened, Linc?*

A screeching alert jarred him awake. Colt checked his phone. He must have fallen asleep thinking about his brother. He wasn't surprised that his exhausted body had succumbed to the stillness while they waited. The community alert that now appeared on his screen had awakened him.

Strong hurricane winds will cause damage and power outages and fallen trees. Take immediate cover.

Jordyn silenced her phone. "Do you think this one is real? Could the BoneDigger be trying to get us out into the open again?"

Bones whined.

"Buddy, it's okay." Colt started the engine. "I'm guessing it's real based on Bones's response. Let's get to the university and we'll check with your dad on the way to confirm." Colt exited the parking lot, taking a right before punching in her father's number.

"Colt, you and Jordyn okay?" her father asked.

"We're good, Dad." Jordyn ran her fingers along the console, grazing Colt's hand. She jerked hers back as if she'd touched a scorching burner.

The simple act stirred Colt's feelings. Could

she also feel the electricity between them? He cleared his throat and stared out the window. Anything to keep his mind off the beautiful woman beside him. "Sir, did you just get a hurricane alert?"

"Yes. Are you at the university?"

"Good, we wanted to be sure it wasn't another hack." Colt pulled onto the main street. "We're heading there now. We'll call when we're there."

"Good." Her father punched off.

Fifteen minutes later, Colt parked in the university parking lot next to the hospital and exited his vehicle.

The trio fought against the wind gusts and the pelting rain as they plodded their way up the steps to the university's main entrance. Colt pried the door open and held it from slamming shut. "Quick. Get inside."

Jordyn hurried into the building with Bones at her heels, and all of a sudden a microphone appeared in front of her face.

"Dr. Miller, is the latest death linked to the kidnapping of your sister?" Ursula Baine pressed. "Have the authorities found her yet?"

Great. If the BoneDigger hadn't realized he'd kidnapped the wrong twin, he would now. Colt gritted his teeth. While he appreciated the determined reporter's quest to get an accurate story for the community, he had to silence her before she put them all in danger.

He placed his hand over the mic. "We have no comment. What are you doing here?"

Bones growled and moved in front of Jordyn, keeping the reporter from advancing.

Ursula backed away. "People have a right to know." She read from her notebook. "Was Wanda Harrelson's death related to the BoneDigger cases?"

How did she know the victim's name? Colt suppressed his anger and fought the urge to march the reporter out of the building. "Miss Baine, we can't comment on an ongoing investigation. How many times do I need to remind you?"

"So you admit *something* is happening in our community?"

Jordyn waggled her finger in Ursula's face. "You need to leave before I have security throw you out. We don't have time for this." She brushed past her.

"What are you hiding, Dr. Miller?" Ursula yelled.

"Bones, guard," Colt commanded his partner.

The dog bolted after Jordyn.

Colt turned to Ursula. "Please leave."

The woman tucked her microphone away and flipped up her hood, securing it tightly. "Fine. But just so you're aware, I will get the scoop on whatever is going on." She hesitated. "Plus, I could be a valuable asset to your investigation. I know things."

Colt straightened. What did that mean? He didn't doubt her words. She had already proved her ability to get to the heart of a story, but did she know something they didn't? "What are you referring to?"

"That's not how this works. You give me an exclusive, and I'll tell you. Think on that, and get back to me." Ursula shoved a business card at Colt, then marched to the entrance and pushed the door open.

The wind blasted into the lobby, and within seconds, rain had soaked the floor.

Colt caught up with Jordyn just as she was walking up to the elevator.

"That woman infuriates me." She punched the up button multiple times.

Colt smirked. "What did that button do to you?"

"Funny." Once the doors opened, she stepped inside. "Sorry, I'm just concerned about my sister." She pointed to the card in his hand. "You have a date with the cute reporter?"

Bones followed her in and sat at her feet.

"Not in a million years. She alluded to knowing something we didn't."

Jordyn's jaw dropped. "We have to talk to her again. She may have a lead on Morgan's disappearance."

Colt fingered the card before stuffing it into

his pocket. "Or it may only be a ploy to get me to open up about the investigation."

"Does Sergeant Warren have any updates on Morgan's kidnapping?"

"No, not yet. However, your father not only has *our* entire force out looking but also *his* personal bodyguards. Even in this storm." Colt pushed the button that would take him to Jordyn's lab. He had visited it numerous times and also attended some of her classes when they were dating. He had enjoyed her lectures on all aspects of anthropology.

The elevator jolted before it lurched upward.

Jordyn lost her footing and fell into his arms.

Her vanilla-scented shampoo wreaked havoc on his emotions and sent a question into his head.

How would he be able to stay close to her without past feelings reemerging?

The sudden nearness of her ex-boyfriend sent Jordyn's heart walloping. Her gaze moved to his lips and his chin dimple. She caught a longing expression passing over his face before it changed to dismissal as he pushed away from her. Their earlier connection in the car entered her mind. The simple act of grazing his hand had been a habit of hers when they were in a relationship, and it still came easily. Too easily. She was tired and hadn't been thinking. She swallowed to clear the thickening in her throat. How could she work with him when all she could think about was kissing him again? *It's clear he's still not interested, Jordyn. Step away.* Plus, her work kept her busy. She didn't have time for any relationships. Now—or ever.

His rejection ten months ago had caused her to throw herself deeper into her career. Anything to help her forget the love they had once shared—or perhaps it had only been one-sided.

The elevator came to a stop, and the doors opened to her floor. *Time to work, Jordyn. Stop fantasizing.*

She avoided Colt and headed toward the autopsy lab, determination squaring her shoulders. She would not think about Colt Peters and his attractive chin dimple. It had always been her kryptonite, but she would erase it from her mind. She had a job to do.

Bones hovered by her side. The dog wasn't letting her out of his sight—one benefit to all this mess. The presence of this amazing animal brought a ray of sunshine to her dreary attitude. She loved dogs and missed Bones's company. She'd thought of getting a dog after Colt severed their relationship, but the thought of the responsibility had been too much. Plus, having one would have reminded her of these two, and she wasn't willing to reopen all the hurt.

She ignored the thoughts from the past, pushed open the doors and entered the state-of-the-art lab. Her father had seen to it that her employers equip the facility with everything possible to do their jobs effectively, and the MEs were grateful for his generosity.

Thoughts of her strained relationship with her father emerged. Ever since she'd asked him about the strange childhood memory she'd had, he treated her differently. *What are you hiding, Dad?* His secret continued to hold their once-strong relationship captive.

Enough reminiscing. Time to get to work.

After texting her father to let him know they had made it safely to the lab, Jordyn set her bag on the table. "Dr. Chambers, you're here already. My team will begin our investigation immediately, as we have lots to do."

"How many times do I have to tell you? Call me Vance." The early thirties man with dark brown eyes gestured toward the evidence bags that had been delivered. "I wanted to see first-hand what we're up against. I'm calling Dr. Jones to bring in more medical examiners. Your father is already pressuring us to finish quickly, so we're going to need their help."

"Totally agree."

Vance turned to Colt. "I'm Dr. Vance Chambers. You are?"

Colt stuck out his hand. "That's right, we haven't met. Constable Colt Peters, K-9 handler from the constabulary. This is my partner, Bones."

Vance chuckled. "Love the name, but why the dog? These are secure premises."

Colt glared at Vance. "Premier Miller requested protection for his daughter."

Jordyn caught the shift in Colt's normally pleasant expression. Why the change? Was it something about Vance? She brushed off her questions and grabbed her lab coat.

"Just ignore me. I'm going to ensure everything is okay here." Colt sauntered around the lab.

Jordyn approached a table and studied the bones.

Vance followed her. "Any preliminary thoughts?"

"Total of five skeletons. One is charred. Two females, three males." Jordyn flipped open her notebook.

"I'll let you continue. I'll be in and out of the lab, but the hurricane has started, so I'll be staying close by." Vance brought his cell phone out of his lab coat pocket. "I'm gonna make that call now. See you later." He left the room.

Colt and Nick both watched the television mounted on the wall on the other side of the room. A meteorologist fought to keep her hood secure while reporting on the weather from outside her station.

"Jezebel has begun her rampage in our region," she yelled over the gusty winds. "As you can see behind me, the heavy rain and winds have already flooded streets. Folks, don't try to go out now. It's too dangerous. Time to hunker down. I'm heading inside. Stay safe." The camera panned across the area before cutting back to the news anchor in the studio.

Nick clicked off the set. "I guess we'll all be staying here for the night. Jordyn, your father had food and provisions sent over."

"That was fast. Sorry I didn't end up getting the pizza. Too much happening." Jordyn's shoulders relaxed. *Thank you, Dad.* His thoughtfulness surprised her but also warmed her heart.

"Food for us and Bones, water, blankets, a doggy bed for Bones, plus cots for us to sleep on." Nick chuckled. "I guess he knows your habit of working long hours."

"He does. Guys, I'm sorry about all this. You can leave if you want to." She hated to inconvenience everyone.

"Not on your life," Eve said. "We're in it for the long haul. Besides, the area is pretty much on lockdown now. No one in or out."

"She's right," Colt said. "It's too dangerous out there. We're in the safest spot."

Woof.

The group laughed.

"Okay, then. Even Bones agrees." She turned to Eve. "Anything on the ages of our victims?"

"That's as far as we got before you returned."

She pointed to their examination area. "I would hazard a—"

Jordyn raised her index finger. "Don't finish your sentence. You know my thoughts. What are they?"

"'Evidence before conclusions,'" Eve and Nick recited together.

"I've taught you well," Jordyn said. "Okay, time to work."

Colt removed his coat and hung it over the back of a chair. He ruffled Bones's ears. "You can rest, boy."

Over the next few hours and into the night, Jordyn led the team in placing the bones in an anatomical position on separate tables, labeling each one. The group worked efficiently, and Jordyn was thankful for their growing knowledge. Eve's eagerness proved she would quickly learn as much as she could. Nick was in his late twenties and had previously trained as a paramedic, so that gave him an edge. The two were the perfect addition to Jordyn's team.

The storm continued to pound the region, and the lights occasionally flickered. Jordyn offered a silent prayer for the electricity to stay on. Not that God listened to her—but her mother had taught her to pray in all circumstances.

Jordyn stole a glimpse at Colt talking on his cell phone. She guessed he was speaking to his sergeant. *Please find Morgan.*

Her own phone buzzed in her pocket. Jordyn peeled off her gloves and fished out the device. Her father. She moved away from the table, then sauntered into the corridor with Bones at her heels. They crossed the hall and stepped inside the lunchroom.

"Hey, Dad. Where are you and Mom?" While Jordyn's relationship with her father was shaky, Fran Miller and Jordyn had a solid bond. Her mother was one of her best friends.

"I'm here, too, sweetheart." Her mother's soothing voice calmed Jordyn's frayed nerves.

"Mom, so good to hear your voice. You guys still at the cottage residence, or did you get out of the region?"

"Not with one daughter missing and the other in danger."

Her father's abrupt tone had the opposite effect on Jordyn.

Her muscles tightened.

"There's no way I can leave when my babies are in danger." Her mom sniffed. Jordyn guessed her softhearted mother was probably blinking back tears.

"Mom, I'm so sorry for all this. It's my fault." Jordyn sank into the couch.

Bones hopped up and curled next to her, laying his head on her lap.

It seemed the dog also needed comfort. Jordyn broke the rules and leaned over, kissing his forehead.

"Young lady, get that idea out of your mind, pronto," her mother said. "The monster who kidnapped Morgan is responsible. Not you."

"Your mother is right, Pooh Bear." Her father's softened voice filtered through the phone. "The storm has hampered the search—but once it's over, every police officer in our area will be searching. I will see to it personally."

Her father's use of the nickname *Pooh Bear* warmed her like a cozy blanket. He'd nicknamed Jordyn after the cute bear and Morgan after Piglet because they were inseparable as kids. He used to joke they stuck together like honey, and the books had been their favorites.

If only she had the same relationship with both Morgan and her father now.

"Thanks, Dad. And thank you for all the provisions. We're grateful."

"Well, I know you, and I know you won't rest until you get the job done. One of the many qualities I admire about you."

Silence filled the lunchroom. She couldn't remember the last time her father had paid her a compliment.

The clock struck six. The darkness outside still hid the early-morning hour. They had worked all night, but she was far from tired. The coffee she'd drank earlier sparked energy throughout her body. Plus, her father was right. She wouldn't rest until she solved the mystery of the unmarked graves.

"How's the examination going?" her mother asked.

"We're getting there. I'm about to determine the—"

An explosion sounded outside, moments before the lights flickered and the electricity died.

The only light that remained came from her cell phone, but the screen revealed the call had dropped.

Bones growled.

A light in the hallway bounced toward them.

Colt appeared in the doorway, his flashlight and weapon raised.

Jordyn jerked upright, popping to her feet. "Colt, what's going on?"

He rushed to the window and opened the blinds. "The storm didn't take out the power."

Streetlights illuminated the parking lot.

Energy left her legs, and she crumbled back onto the couch. Her body's previously charged strength had dissipated.

Had the BoneDigger found them and plunged them into complete darkness, leaving them helpless?

SEVEN

"Jordyn!" Colt holstered his Sig and sprinted to her side. Her ashen face revealed that his news had shattered her sense of safety there in the lab. Was this the BoneDigger's doing? Colt brushed the stray brown hair off her face and tucked it behind her ear. "You okay?"

Bones had repositioned himself on the other side of her, keeping watch through the darkness.

She pulled away from Colt's touch. "I'll be fine. What happened? Why is our power out but not everywhere else?"

"Don't know. I wanted to make sure you're okay." Colt unclipped his shoulder radio. "I'll check with Constable Greer outside. Sergeant Warren sent her here to guard us." He pushed the talk button. "Greer, report. Why is the electricity off in the building?"

"Checking it out now and securing the perimeter." Her voice was uneven, which told him she was jogging. "I'll report back when I have more details."

"Copy that." Colt helped Jordyn to her feet. "Let's gather the others. Safety in numbers."

"Do you think the BoneDigger did this? How did—"

The lights flipped back on.

Jordyn pumped her fist. "Yes! Our building's generator kicked in. We can keep working."

"You've worked nonstop for the past few days. Shouldn't you rest?" He pointed to the cots on the other side of the room.

"Have to call Mom for a second." She punched in a number on her cell phone and peered over at him. "Are you kidding? I can't sleep now—I need answers. Maybe something locked in these victims' bones will help reveal exactly who the BoneDigger is and where he's taken my sister." She left the lunchroom.

Bones barked and trotted after her.

"Jordyn! Wait up." How could she leave her protective detail behind so easily? Shouldn't the premier's daughter know better?

Thankfully, Colt had trained Bones well. He would stay by her side.

At least she didn't mind the dog's company. Colt's, however, was a different story. He remembered how she'd recoiled from his touch just moments before. She still hated him for breaking her heart.

She had every right, of course. He should never have gotten involved, but he couldn't resist her beauty and sweet personality when they'd first met. Guilt over failing Linc consumed him. There was no way he could get so close to someone again and risk making the same mistakes. Linc had not only been his brother but also his best friend.

He remembered a saying his father had ingrained in them when they were young. *Friends don't desert each other.* The brothers had done everything together. They had even chosen the same college—but Linc never got the chance to graduate. He'd shared with Colt how he wanted to become a paramedic and save lives.

Why did the guilt still haunt Colt after ten years?

You know why.

He had not only failed Linc but also his entire family by deserting his brother that day—something his mother had never let him forget. Colt had tried to stay in touch, but she refused to even look at him. His father had told him she'd said his presence reminded her too much of her loss. Her heart had been broken.

Nothing they'd done had helped heal Abigail Peters.

Not even You, God. Why? Did You desert Mom?

Colt entered the lab and studied the five sets of bones lying in anatomical order on top of a black photo tarp on each table.

Colt squared his shoulders as a resolution hit him.

This is how I help steer Mom onto the healing

road. Solve Linc's suspicious death so his family could have closure. He needed it—and his mom definitely did too.

Lord, make it so.

Bones had positioned himself as close to Jordyn as he could get without getting in her way. Smart dog.

Colt approached. "How long will your examination take?"

Jordyn peered at him over the top of her medical protective glasses. "Too long. After I finish each skeleton, I'll pass my findings and documentation on to Vance. Then he'll begin his investigation." Her gaze traveled over to Eve and Nick.

They smirked.

"What am I missing here?" Colt asked.

"Nothing. Dr. Chambers is an odd duck." Jordyn adjusted her medical gloves. "But he's good at what he does."

Eve chuckled. "And he has a crush on Jordyn."

Jordyn shook her head. "Hardly."

Nick tsk-tsked. "Well, he got us a new CT scanner. Doesn't that tell you something?"

"My father provided that. Dr. Chambers just highly recommended one for the lab."

Jealousy stirred in Colt's gut. Why? It was not like Jordyn would take him back, anyway. Time to change the subject. "What can I do?"

She pointed to another table. "Forensics dusted

the lynx carvings for prints, so how about you grab gloves and inspect them. Perhaps you'll find a clue as to why the BoneDigger made them."

Greer's voice suddenly filtered through his radio. "Peters, you there?"

Colt pressed the talk button. "You got something?"

"I'm here with the premier's men. Someone cut the hydro leading into the building."

Colt's muscles tensed, and he reached for his sidearm—an automatic response to danger. "Secure the premises. Scour the perimeter. Find this person."

"Already on it. Just wanted to give you an update." Shouts sounded in the background. "Someone spotted something. We'll check it out, but be on alert."

"Will do." Colt turned to Jordyn. "I'm going to ensure we're locked in."

"Are we okay?" Her normally steady voice shook with trepidation.

"Whoever did this will have to get through both the constabulary and your father's men." Colt addressed the others. "Don't worry. My partner is the best." He patted Bones's back. "Right, buddy?"

Bones barked.

"Guard," Colt commanded.

The dog inched closer to Jordyn.

Colt locked the doors to the lab and the entire

floor. He returned to the room and stared out a window. "We're good, but it looks nasty out there." He inspected the building facing the autopsy lab. A shadow passed by a window. What—

A rush of wind slapped tree branches against the glass. He startled from the sudden noise, his heart pounding. Colt snuck another peek, but whatever he had seen in the other building was gone. He scanned the property below, but the heavy rains now pounded the hospital and university grounds, obstructing his view. If someone was out there, he wouldn't see their approach. It must have been his imagination. There was no way anyone would brave the fierce storm. Still…

Were they safe inside the building? From both Jezebel and the BoneDigger? Had he followed them?

The wind howled as if in response and sent shivers shooting down his back. How long until Jezebel finished wreaking havoc on their region?

Bones barked, pulling Colt's attention back to the room. He moved over to his partner's side and squatted, rubbing the dog's back. "It's okay, bud. The storm will pass."

"Colt, be on alert," Greer said through the radio. "Found the maintenance worker gagged and secured in a closet. Says he was knocked out and his uniform stolen."

Panic zinged through Colt's body. Had the

BoneDigger gained access to the building and cut the power to get close to them?

Now it was up to Colt to keep them safe.

Jordyn analyzed Colt. Even though they'd only dated for a few months, she knew that look. Something had rattled him. "What's going on?"

"Not sure." Colt pressed the talk button on his radio. "Greer, thought I saw movement in the building across from us. Do a double-check to be sure."

"On it."

"Are we okay?" Jordyn asked.

"Greer is doing another sweep. We're locked in, so we're good." He returned to the table where they'd placed the lynx carvings and put on medical gloves. "Back to work."

Don't believe you. Jordyn steeled her jaw. He had the same expression when he'd broken up with her. She had asked why, and he had simply said he no longer loved her. She'd sensed that he was leaving something out. There was more to his story. Then…and now.

But she let it go. For now.

She required caffeine. "Eve, did Dad send my favorite coffee?"

Her trainee guffawed. "Of course, but you'll have to brew some. I made regular since you're the only one who likes that pumpkin spice stuff."

Jordyn didn't understand why people scoffed

at the fall flavor. What wasn't to like? She pondered this as she made her way to their lounge and brewed a full pot. Her weary bones told her she needed it.

After pouring herself a large mug, she added cream and made her way back into the lab. She sipped. "Ah, now *that's* excellent coffee." She glanced at Colt.

He smirked and shook his head, then returned to studying the carvings.

She swallowed the emerging emotions and focused her attention back on the scene before her. Skeletons placed on five separate tables.

Not a normal sight in their lab. They usually only had one or two sets—three at the most. Five was unheard of in their small community.

"Nick, did you print the pictures we took at the graveyard?" she asked.

"Yes, I put each set on the side tables by the corresponding skeletons." He pointed to the fifty-two-inch monitor. "I used the points of interest from the survey equipment to create a digital map. It's on the screen."

"Exceptional work." Her trainees were the best. That was why she'd chosen them.

She approached the monitor and scrutinized the Charock Cemetery lot and where they'd dug for their extended plot.

The unmarked graves they'd uncovered were

farther into the tree line, but one was close enough that someone had found it. *Wait...*

She pivoted and almost bumped into Bones. "Sorry, bud. Forgot you were right beside me."

He barked.

Jordyn resisted the urge to bend down and kiss his head. *Oh, how I've missed you, Bones.* The pair had enjoyed many evenings snuggled up on the couch, watching the roaring fire during the winter months. Bones had loved to sit next to her in the comfy, rustic living room.

Now only silence remained in her log-style home. Some days were unbearable. It was why she worked so hard—she couldn't face evenings alone.

Don't go there again. She braced herself, refusing to revisit past regrets, and turned back to the monitor. "Colt, do we know who discovered the grave and called in the anonymous tip?"

"The digital forensics team reported they were able to trace it back to a young teen who claims he was out with his buddies, doing drugs. That's why he wouldn't give his identity. Didn't want to get caught." He looked up. "Why?"

She pointed to the screen. "This is the first grave I examined. The one the tipster called in. It's away from the cemetery—but how did they find it in the dark?"

"The teens must have had flashlights," Eve offered.

Jordyn tapped her chin. "Maybe. Just seems like an odd place to do drugs. But who knows these days?"

"Agreed," Colt said.

Jordyn clapped. "Okay, let's get back to work." While her team worked at the far tables, she moved toward the table that held the remains she felt strongly were Lincoln's.

You don't identify—you're the eyes. Tell us what you see.

Her chief ME's words thundered in her brain. Dr. Jones had instilled his mantra in all his employees.

Right. She didn't know for sure these were Lincoln's bones, but the ring they'd found made it very possible.

For Colt's sake, she prayed she was right. She knew guilt still haunted him.

Colt approached her table and stopped. "These Linc's?"

"We don't know definitively." She placed her hand on his arm. "The ME will confirm for sure."

Sadness glistened in his eyes. "Is it wrong for me to want them to be Linc's?"

"No, Colt. You and your parents need closure."

"Police stopped investigating too quickly back then. Said Linc probably intentionally left the area, but I know that's not true. No way he'd leave Mom." Colt's lips curved upward. "He was a mama's boy."

Dizziness suddenly attacked Jordyn, and her vision blurred. She grasped the table's edge to steady herself.

"You okay?" Colt asked.

Jordyn inhaled and exhaled slowly until the wooziness passed. "I'm fine. Probably too much caffeine and not enough food."

"I saw some muffins in the lunchroom. You have to eat." He paused. "And sleep."

"No time for that. I want to get a lot done today. Remember our time crunch."

Rain pounded the window as another massive wind gust rattled the glass, underscoring her comment.

A shudder tightened her muscles. *This storm will eventually cut all power. Lord, please make Jezebel pass over us quickly.*

Not that God was listening.

He had left her alone—in the darkness.

Colt's cell phone dinged, and after taking a look at the screen, he sucked in a breath.

Jordyn's pulse escalated at the frantic expression on his face. "What is it?"

Bones pranced around Jordyn and Colt as if sensing the shift in his handler's disposition.

Colt eyed Eve and Nick, then returned his attention to Jordyn. "Can we talk in your lunchroom?"

"Of course." Something told Jordyn she would not like what Colt had to say, but she forced her weary legs forward, following him into the lunchroom.

Bones remained by her side.

He closed the door.

Not good.

Colt pointed to the doggy bed. “Bones, stay.”

The dog trotted over to the oval cushion and circled it before curling up on top.

Jordyn latched on to Colt’s arm. “You’re scaring me. What happened?”

“Got a text from someone claiming to be the BoneDigger.” He handed her his phone.

A picture of Morgan, gagged and tied to a cot in some sort of dungeon, was on the screen, accompanied by a deadly message.

Stop your investigation or Dr. Miller’s sister will die.
—BoneDigger

Jordyn gasped. “No!”

The BoneDigger had realized he had kidnapped the wrong twin, and now Morgan would pay the price.

The room spun, intensifying her dizziness and overwhelming her body with a wave of nausea. Panic set in, and she reached for the table but missed.

A dog’s bark registered in the background as her knees buckled and the darkness lured her into a black hole.

EIGHT

"No!" Colt dropped beside Jordyn and placed his fingers on her neck, checking for a pulse. Strong. Had she only fainted from exhaustion? He wasn't aware of any medical conditions. Or was it the shock of seeing her sister tied and gagged? Colt touched her forehead with the back of his hand. Clammy.

Bones barked and licked Jordyn's face. Seemed he, too, wanted to revive his charge.

"Guys, help!" Colt had done a quick check on both Eve and Nick to be sure they were legit, and so he knew that Nick had a paramedic background.

Jordyn wouldn't like that he'd done that, but Colt couldn't take any risks with her welfare.

Pounding footfalls alerted him to their presence.

Nick kneeled by Jordyn's side. "What happened?"

Colt moved out of the way. "She fainted. She

was dizzy earlier. You have a medical background—can you check her out?"

Nick addressed Eve. "Grab the first-aid kit. It's on the wall in the lab."

"Please help her." Eve's voice quivered. "She's like a big sister to me." She hurried from the room.

Nick checked Jordyn's pulse and examined her limbs. "Nothing stands out to me. Are you aware if she's on any meds for high blood pressure?"

"Not to my knowledge." Colt pulled out his cell phone and punched in her mother's number. He knew how close she was to Fran. "Her mom would know. Let me check."

"You're still on good terms with her family?"

"Kind of." He pushed himself up and paced as he waited for her to pick up.

Fran Miller answered on the second ring. "Hey, Colt. Is Jordyn okay?"

"I don't want to worry you, but she fainted."

"What? Did you call for an ambulance?" Fran's voice quivered.

"Nick was a paramedic. He's looking at her right now. Can you tell us if she's on any meds? Perhaps for high blood pressure?"

A sigh sailed through the phone. "Yes. Russell doesn't know. She wouldn't let me tell him." Silence followed. "Her stress level had increased, so her doctor put her on them. But only a low dosage. They probably wouldn't make her faint.

If I know her—and I do—she hasn't eaten much for the past few days. When she's on a case, she ignores her own needs."

Eve returned to the office, carrying the first-aid kit. She dropped beside Nick and opened the case.

Nick pointed. "Grab the smelling salts."

"I'm sure that's it." Colt returned to the group. "Okay, thanks. We're going to try smelling salts."

"Please ask her to call me," Fran said.

"Will do."

"And, Colt... She works too hard. She's gone to a dark place in the past few months. I can see it in her eyes and demeanor, even though she tries to hide it." The woman's voice cracked. "I'm concerned."

That was probably his fault since he'd broken her heart.

Colt set aside the thought and crouched next to Jordyn. "Thanks for your help. Try not to worry." He clicked off the call. "Okay, she's on blood pressure meds. Could that have done this?"

"Perhaps." Nick waved the salts in front of Jordyn's nose.

Within seconds, she coughed and opened her eyes. "What happened?" She tried to sit up but fell back down.

"Take it easy," Colt said. "You fainted. Did you forget to take your blood pressure pills?"

"Or take too many?" Nick added.

"No, but how did…" She pursed her lips. "You called Mom."

Colt knew she'd be upset about him interfering. She was a private person and didn't like some things advertised. "We had to determine why you fainted."

She raised herself up on her elbows. "Help me up, guys."

Colt and Nick guided her to the couch.

"Did you eat anything yesterday?" Colt asked.

Jordyn shot him a *Did you just ask me that?* look. "Yes, *Mom.* And I took my meds. It's not that." Jordyn held her head. "The room is spinning again."

"Lay back," Nick said. "Tell me your symptoms."

"Light-headed and feverish."

Nick turned to the group. "Anyone else feeling this way?"

Eve shook her head.

"No." Colt racked his brain, trying to determine the cause.

"Me neither." Nick felt her forehead. "You're clammy, but you don't have a fever. Maybe something you ate?"

"We all ate the same muffins." Colt eyed the coffeepot and bristled. "Wait—did any of you drink her pumpkin spice coffee?"

Eve turned up her nose. "Hate the stuff."

"Not me. What are you thinking?" Nick asked.

"Maybe someone laced the coffee grounds with

another drug that interacted with her meds." Colt clenched his fists. "Who delivered the food?"

Had the BoneDigger somehow gotten to them?

"A delivery service." Nick turned to Eve. "Our normal one, right?"

Eve's eyes widened. "No. The driver said the company passed it to them because the storm put them out of commission. This guy got here just before the worst part of the hurricane started."

Something didn't add up.

"You're thinking the BoneDigger did this?" Jordyn asked. "It can't be true. I probably just need sleep."

"Nothing is off the table right now. I don't trust the fact that your normal driver didn't come. Just sounds too convenient." Colt's cell phone buzzed. He checked the screen.

How's the doc doing? Don't worry, she'll be okay. Just gave her coffee an extra kick to prove how close I can get to both of you...and her team. Back off. —BD.

Colt whistled. "I was right. It was the Bone-Digger."

Jordyn clutched the sofa's armrest. "How do you know?"

He raised his phone. "He just admitted it."

She leaned closer. "How did he know Dad ordered these provisions, though?" She grabbed his arm. "Wait, could Dad's security detail be leaking information? Ted and Oscar are the best at what they do. I can't imagine they'd double-cross my dad."

"Possibly, but I'm sure your father vetted them personally." Colt rubbed his temples, attempting to massage away an oncoming headache. "Anything's possible in this day and age, with technology the way it is."

"My dad will be furious."

"Jordyn, call your mom. She's worried." Colt gestured to the group. "She's going to be okay. Let's leave her alone and give her privacy. I'm going to look at those carvings. They may hold some answers that will solve this case and find the BoneDigger." He turned to his partner. "Bones, stay."

Right now, his K-9 was the only one Colt trusted to keep Jordyn safe.

In the meantime, he would discard any food transported by the unknown delivery truck. He didn't want to risk that anything else had been contaminated.

The earlier text entered his mind, leaving Colt with a question.

How was the BoneDigger able to get so close to them?

Jordyn poured herself a glass of water to quench her thirst and willed strength into her weary muscles. Her fingers shook as she drank before placing the glass on the table. She clenched her hands to stop the trembles. What had he put in that coffee? *God, what else will You allow?* Jordyn bit her lip and pushed aside thoughts of an unseen entity. She had to deal with the here and now. She pulled her cell phone from her pocket and hit the speed dial button for her mother.

She answered on the first ring. "Jordyn! Are you okay?"

"I will be. Just drinking some water to get some fluids." Jordyn sat on the couch and patted the cushion next to her, inviting Bones to come up. She realized she was breaking protocol, but she didn't care.

What did it matter right now?

The dog jumped up and snuggled beside her.

"What happened?" her mother asked.

Jordyn rubbed Bones's ear. "Someone added something to my coffee, but I'm fine."

"Who would do that?"

"Colt is looking into it." How much should she tell her? Her mother was a worrywart, and Jordyn hated to add to her anxiety. She already had enough happening with Morgan's kidnapping. Time to change the subject. "Are you and Dad safe from the storm?"

"His men have battened down the hatches, as they say." Her voice broke. "I'm scared, Jordyn. We have to find Morgan. Ginny and Pepper are frantic and need their mother. Tyler is on his way back from his business trip overseas."

Jordyn pictured her nieces and their bright red curls bouncing as they played hopscotch in the driveway. The family wasn't sure where they'd inherited their hair color but guessed it had come from Tyler's side. Even though Jordyn and Morgan's relationship had been strained, she still loved the girls.

Time to move on.

Words her mother said to Jordyn often. Jordyn knew she was right. She'd harbored the pain for far too long. It was time to put it behind her.

Once and for all.

"Jordyn, you still there?" her mother asked.

The question brought her back to their conversation. "Sorry. Colt is determined to help find Morgan. He's good at his job."

"And good for you."

Jordyn cringed. "Don't go there, Mom. He broke my heart for no apparent reason."

"Well, there's obviously something he's not telling you. Perhaps now is the time to find out." A pause. "You were the happiest you've ever been when you guys were together."

She rubbed Bones's fur. Her mother wasn't wrong—Jordyn and Colt had clicked instantly. More so than she and Tyler ever had. She'd met Colt at a joint meeting with other law enforcement and forensic members. Colt had asked her out the next day, and they were inseparable after that. Until…

They weren't.

Jordyn gripped the cell phone tighter. "Mom, I can guess what's going through that brain of yours. Colt and I won't be getting back together. He's made that very clear. Besides, I'm too busy for any relationship."

"Love, you work too hard. You're young and have lots of life yet to live. Don't waste any time. We just don't know what tomorrow brings."

Woof!

"I hear Bones. So glad your father sent him and Colt to protect you. Love…you need…come… the Lord."

Her mother's broken words were lost.

"Mom?"

The line went silent.

Jordyn rose slowly and shuffled to the window. The wind and rain had intensified. Jezebel had worsened. She guessed the hurricane had taken out the nearby cell tower, cutting them off from the outside world.

Jordyn dropped her phone into her lab jacket and turned to Bones. "Come."

Colt had taught her how to give his partner the common commands. Bones obeyed and followed her out into the lab.

Eve hurried to her side. "You okay?"

"Still somewhat weak, but I'll be fine." She approached Colt. "I just lost cell phone reception."

"Great," Nick said. "That's all we need."

"Not good." Colt extracted his police-issued phone and grimaced. "No bars. What about the landline?"

Nick snatched the phone from the wall, tapping the receiver button. "Nothing." He slammed it back onto its cradle.

"One good thing is, the BoneDigger can't contact us now, so we can concentrate on our examinations. Back to it, friends." Jordyn inched closer to Colt so the others wouldn't hear her question. "What do we do now? I don't trust the food Dad provided."

"Agreed. I already threw it out. I did request Greer inquire about replacement food, but it's hard to say if she'll be able to in this weather. Do you have anything in the staff fridge or vending machines?"

She raised her index finger. "Yes, some leftovers. And there are chips, chocolate bars and other snacks in the vending machine in the hallway."

"You always loved your chocolate bars." He winked.

Don't do that to me, Colt. I'm already having a hard time resisting your smile. She averted her gaze to the window. "I'm not sure how long the generator will last."

Colt addressed Nick. "Turn the TV on while we still have power. Let's get a weather update."

Nick hit a button on the remote, and the meteorologist's face appeared amid rain pounding sideways. The wind whisked her hood off, and she struggled to keep it on her head. "Folks, as you can see, Jezebel is right on top of us. The good news is, they've downgraded it to a Category 2. But please, stay inside."

"Finally, some good news." Nick clicked off the TV.

"Yes. Let's keep working, shall we?" Jordyn returned to the bones she suspected were Lincoln's. "We have to get our assessments done. Eve, clean up the charred remains like I taught you."

Eve hesitated, panic settling over her face. "Are you sure?"

"You've got this, Eve. I believe in you." Jordyn had taken the young woman under her wing the first time they met. The two had clicked. Jordyn saw herself in Eve. She hated to lose her but knew she would eventually, as the job would one day take her across the country and possibly to New York.

Jordyn herself had relocated to three provinces and trained in New York for a few years before returning to Newfoundland—the land she loved.

"Thanks, boss." Eve gathered her tools and moved to another station.

Over the next two hours, Jordyn examined the bones she strongly believed were Colt's brother's.

She studied the frontal bone with her microscopic tool. "What the..."

"What is it?" Nick asked.

"Look at this." She handed him the tool. "I want your take on it. Could it be ballistic trauma?"

Colt walked up to her table. "You find something?"

"Maybe." She addressed Nick. "What do you think?"

"Definitely consistent with a GSW." He returned to his table. "I just found the same thing on this skull. Look."

Jordyn rushed over to the other male skeleton and focused on where Nick was pointing. "Agreed, but this time, it's at the base of the skull." Jordyn took off her gloves and grabbed her tablet. "I would guess this shot came as the victim ran away."

"Thought you didn't guess," Nick said.

"Let me rephrase—this ballistic trauma is consistent with a shot coming from behind the victim."

Colt's jaw dropped. "Linc was shot too?" He stared at the bones.

"If this is indeed Lincoln, yes—I believe so. I will add it to the documentation for Dr. Chambers to decide. He will officially determine the cause of death, but from close inspection…" She pointed to the skull. "That's a GSW."

They definitely had a serial killer on the loose. The question was…would he strike again?

NINE

Colt stumbled backward and almost tripped over Bones. He had failed to see his partner's approach. The dog had obviously sensed Colt's trepidation over Jordyn's conclusions regarding Linc's death. Colt flopped down into a nearby chair and cradled his head in his hands. He hated to show his emotion, but he'd stored ten years of wondering what had happened to his brother, and Jordyn had just punctured the proverbial balloon, releasing the air. His heartstrings tumbled out, and he lost control. Not his typical constable persona.

Jordyn placed her hand on his shoulder. "Colt, we still don't know 100 percent that this is Linc."

His head whipped up. "We do. My gut is telling me it is. How long before we can get your documentation to Dr. Chambers? I need confirmation before I tell my parents."

"Well, I'm going to send him my findings on this one, and he'll probably send a request for dental records to verify the identity. He'll determine the cause of death, even though it's pretty obvious it's the GSW. But I don't want to assume."

Colt wrung his hands as if trying to release his anger and guilt over what had happened to his brother. If that was possible. "Why would anyone shoot my brother, specifically the BoneDigger?"

"No idea. I never knew Lincoln, but from what you've told me, everyone loved him."

"I have to find out why the BoneDigger—if it was him—killed Linc." Colt brushed off his guilt and pushed to standing, squaring his shoulders. Yes, he'd find justice for Linc and his parents, even if he had to put himself in a killer's crosshairs. *I owe Linc that much.* "That reminds me—I want to show you something on these wood carvings."

"What did you find?" Jordyn asked as she followed, with Bones at her heels.

Colt put on gloves and lifted a carving. "I've come to some assumptions about the artist."

"Like what?"

"This is an excellent replica of the Canada lynx." He tapped the wood. "Look at the details in the carving. This person is meticulous."

"Definitely."

Colt picked up a magnifying glass, hovering it over the wood. "I found words etched at the bottom. When you look at it with the human eye, it only looks like part of the carving."

She stepped closer and peered through the eyeglass. "No way."

"I wanted to check to see if they all say the same thing." Colt inspected a different carving closely before moving on to the others. "Yup. They do."

Leviticus 27:29.

"What does that verse say?" Jordyn scrunched her nose. "My childhood memories of Bible sword drills are rusty."

Did she know how cute she looked when she crinkled her nose? *Focus, Colt.* "Just a sec." He drew out his cell phone and clicked on his Bible app. "Here we go. It says, 'None devoted, which shall be devoted of men, shall be redeemed; but shall surely be put to death.'"

Jordyn's mouth dropped open. "Is he saying these victims were unredeemable and deserved death?"

Colt examined the skeletons. "What could they have done that was so terrible—especially Linc?"

"No idea. But all this still doesn't help us identify the BoneDigger."

Colt raised his index finger. "No, but I'd requested a trace on the cell phone number he used and got an email earlier. I haven't had a chance to check it. Maybe we got a hit." He retrieved his cell phone and swiped the screen to read the email. "Just as I figured—he's using a burner phone."

"Why am I not surprised?"

"Right?" Colt lined up all the carvings. "I noticed one other thing about the wood. Do you see it?"

Jordyn inspected them but shook her head. "What?"

Colt picked one up from the table. "The wood is new." He pointed to the remains. "I'm guessing these bones have been in the graves for a long period. Linc for ten years."

"Good point." She addressed Nick. "I realize the ME will give us a range, but what's your gut feeling about how long your victim has been deceased?"

Nick tilted his head and winked. "You're asking me to guess? That's so not like you."

She raised her hands. "I know, I know. Humor me."

Nick directed his attention back to the bones. "This female is between seventy and seventy-five. Come and look at this."

Jordyn moved over to his side. "What do you see?"

Colt followed to get a good look too.

Nick pointed to the skeleton's neck. "Check the superior-horn area."

Jordyn studied it using a magnifying tool. "Take pictures of this. I need to look closer, but it appears to be consistent with manual strangulation. Of course, we can't rule out other forms of neck trauma. Dr. Chambers will confirm the cause of death."

"Agreed." Nick tapped his finger on his chin. "So the bones are fully skeletonized and have stains from the environment. I would say this person has possibly been deceased for maybe fifteen to twenty years."

Jordyn paced around the tables. "That doesn't make sense. That would mean—"

"The remains were moved, and the carvings were added after the fact," Colt cut in, finishing her sentence. Something they used to do frequently when they were together.

Jordyn returned to her documentation and flipped through the pages. "Constable Lavigne told me the funeral home had started to dig a new plot line." She glanced up from her notes. "Perhaps the BoneDigger heard about this and panicked."

"He dug up the remains and moved them for fear of discovery." Colt joined Jordyn at her table. "When he reburied them, perhaps he put the carvings in their hand. Not that we know that for sure, of course."

She crossed her arms. "But why?"

"Perhaps claiming his kill and adding a signature, like many serial killers. What I don't understand is, why not move them farther away?"

"Maybe he didn't have time." Eve placed her

brush on her table. "This victim appears to have a GSW to the skull as well."

"That's now three with ballistic trauma." Jordyn plunked herself down in a chair. "Seems that is the BoneDigger's MO—gunshot to the head. My question is, though, why not shoot the older female victim?" She rubbed her temples.

"Perhaps it was a crime of passion? Or the killer evolved into taking the easy way out, wanting to eliminate them quicker." Colt checked the time on his phone. "It's 7:00 p.m. Have you eaten anything?"

"No."

"There are some sandwiches in the fridge." Eve hurried from the room.

Wind rattled the windows, reminding Colt of the dangerous hurricane. *Lord, help it to end soon so we can get our findings to the appropriate people and stop the BoneDigger from killing again.*

Jordyn yawned.

Colt peeled off his gloves and inched closer to her side. "You need rest, or you're gonna drop."

"We have to finish—"

Another gust of wind thrust a large branch into the window, shattering the glass to pieces.

Seconds later, the lights snapped off.

Bones growled.

The knob to the locked lab door jiggled.

Not only had they been plunged into total darkness...but someone was trying to breach their secure area.

* * *

The pounding in Jordyn's head sent dread through her body. She turned on her cell phone's flashlight, illuminating the room. Both Bones and Colt had reacted, braced in a protective stance against whoever was at the door. Wind blew in through the broken window and chilled the room instantly, swirling their documentation around the lab. She had to save the papers from being blown out the shattered window. However, the tension hijacking the room cemented her in her tracks.

Bones inched closer to the door and growled, baring his teeth.

"Bones, silence." Colt's whispered command restrained his partner and everyone in the room. He raised his index finger to his lips, reinforcing his intent.

Keep their presence a secret to the intruder.

If that was possible.

Jordyn held her breath as the wind sent chills up her back.

Colt gestured for her to turn her cell phone flashlight off and bowed his head.

Was he praying the intruder away? Jordyn shut off the light, sending the room back into darkness.

Would God listen to Colt?

The door rattled again as a beam of light bounced through the cracks.

Jordyn shuddered and shook as panic consumed her body. The darkness haunted her. She stumbled backward, bumping into a table holding one set of remains. The events of the past few days snowballed and hit her with the force of a race car, sending her to a place she'd wanted to avoid.

The shadows.

She'd been there too often lately, and becoming a workaholic was the only way to claw herself from the abyss. But now, the attempts on her life and Morgan's abduction threatened to send her back into the murkiness.

Her heart palpitated, increasing her panicked state. She clutched the side of the table with a viselike grip to keep herself from falling. *Breathe, Jordyn, breathe.* In. Out. In. Out.

God, where are You? I have to see Your light.

The rattling continued. The room remained still.

A verse from her childhood emerged…

I am the light of the world.

Was God reaching out to her in a time of need?

Jordyn closed her eyes. Images of Morgan filled her mind, and she longed to hug her twin. Tell her she loved her. It *was* time to move on. They needed each other. Life was too short, and Jordyn hated the bitterness that had consumed her every waking moment. It was long overdue. Plus, didn't God tell them to forgive? Yes.

I forgive you, Morgan.

She prayed for the Lord to help her save her sister from the BoneDigger's clutches. She had to find her.

Her finger grazed a bone, and she stiffened.

Was this how God was telling her to get out of the darkness? By helping these victims? Providing the best possible observations to help find the killer? Perhaps her earlier conclusion was correct—a secret among the bones would unlock the BoneDigger's identity.

She rolled her shoulders back as determination changed her fear to resolution.

Bones rubbed up against her legs protectively. Had Colt taught him this move, or was it instinct for the German shepherd? His presence ushered forth a ripple of peace, calming her disposition.

You've got this.

Footsteps pounded in the corridor outside their door, then slowly grew fainter. The intruder had left. Jordyn exhaled slowly.

They were safe.

For now.

Colt placed his ear against the door. "Sounds like they gave up."

Jordyn turned her cell phone's flashlight back on. "Everyone, find the rest of the flashlights. Even if we have to come to our conclusions by limited lighting, we will. We need to find this killer."

The team scattered in their quest to find additional lighting and soon had them set up over the lab.

Trickles of light brought brightness into the darkness bit by bit and gave her a renewed sense of purpose. Was it from God? She wasn't totally sure yet, but she'd take it.

She gestured toward the window. "Nick, can you find something to keep out the wind?"

He nodded and left the lab.

"Colt, can you check with Sara to see if she got food?"

He spoke into his radio, asking his fellow constable for an update. She stated she'd been too busy fighting the storm and searching for the intruder.

Eve dashed into the room, returning with leftover sandwiches.

Jordyn snagged a sandwich and took a bite.

Colt squeezed her hand. "You good?"

"We need to keep going, Colt. For Linc. For these victims." Jordyn picked up her pen. "Can you hold the light so I can continue documenting?"

"Of course."

Three hours later, Jordyn wiped her dry eyes. Working with restricted lighting had strained them, but she had pressed forward and finished her assessment on the remains she believed to be Lincoln's.

But the others would have to wait until morning. She sent the team to get a few hours of rest, and it was time for her to practice what she preached. Her tired limbs and eyes required much-needed sleep, or she'd drop. "Colt, I'm going to grab a couple hours of shut-eye on the lunchroom sofa. You should rest too."

"I'll be fine. I'll bring a comfy chair to the lunchroom and position myself there. First, let me go secure the hallway and check in with Greer." Colt unhooked his shoulder radio. He turned to his partner and gestured toward Jordyn. "Bones, heel."

Jordyn left the lab with her protector by her side. But would she be able to sleep with a maniac lurking in the shadows?

A scraping noise jarred Colt from his restless slumber, and he bolted upright. His watch read 5:30 a.m. He hadn't meant to fall asleep, but his weary body had had other plans. *Stupid, Colt.* He suppressed his self-criticism and listened for whatever noise had woken him, thankful that something did. Colt wouldn't leave the team unguarded while they slept. He'd stationed himself by the lunchroom door. He praised God that Bones remained at Jordyn's side. She was fast asleep, but Bones sat there, alert and ready to protect her from danger. Just like Colt had trained him to do. His partner was the best of the best. No other could compare—at least, not in Colt's eyes.

Bones was family. Even his mother had warmed up to the dog's magnetism. He had helped fill the void of her younger son's absence.

Colt had brought Bones to visit his mother regularly, even though she didn't want to be in Colt's presence. It was the least he could do after causing this rift between them. He would spend the evenings with his father as his mom enjoyed her Bones time. She spoiled the dog with bones—her way of getting him to live up to his name.

And Bones loved it.

The scraping sounded again, interrupting Colt's thoughts.

A shadow passed under the door.

Colt rested his hand on his weapon and inched closer to the wall, positioning himself to the side of the steel entrance.

Bones barked.

Something had alerted the K-9 to danger.

Then Colt smelled what his dog must have.

Smoke.

Seconds later, the fire alarm shrieked.

Colt turned his flashlight on. "Everyone, get up. Fire!"

Jordyn stumbled off the couch, falling to the floor.

He grabbed her under the arm, ushering her toward the door.

Eve and Nick had each been sleeping on cots in the corner. They bolted to their feet.

"The bones!" Jordyn yelled. "We have to get back to the lab."

"Let me go first." Colt shined his light on the door and eased his fingers onto the handle. It was cool. So where was the fire?

Suspicion prickled, and he grabbed his radio. "Greer, any signs of a fire?"

"We're…checking…now." Her breathless words indicated she was running. "Wait…there."

Bones barked.

Colt struggled to determine a plan of action.

Bones barked again, louder. He pranced around the group and moved over to the door. Turning his gaze back to them, he barked.

Colt unholstered his Sig. "Okay, stay behind me. We're leaving."

"But shouldn't we wait?" Eve asked.

Bones growled.

"I trust my dog, and he's telling us to go." Colt eased opened the door, raising his gun and flashlight simultaneously.

The hall was empty.

"Bones, guard!" Colt held the door fully open.

The German shepherd burst through the entrance, his intent clear…

Secure the area and lead the group to safety.

TEN

Jordyn covered her ears to block the piercing fire alarm as she followed Colt out of the lunchroom. Anxiety had replaced her earlier peaceful attitude, and she chewed on her lip to keep from slipping back into the darkness. *Focus. You're okay. Colt and Bones will keep you and the others safe.*

The group made their way across the hall.

Bones stopped in front of the lab door and barked.

"What is it, boy?" Colt moved closer to his partner. "He's alerting to something."

Jordyn spied the cracked-open door and turned to Nick. "Didn't you secure the door?"

His eyes widened. "I did."

Colt raised his Sig. "Stay here." He inched through the entrance.

Jordyn followed, ignoring his earlier command. She had to ensure the remains were safe.

Bones tugged on the hem of her blouse.

Colt pivoted, gun poised. He lowered his weapon. "Jordyn! I told you to stay in the hall."

"I have to make sure the skeletons are okay." She proceeded farther into the room but stopped.

Flames spat out from under the five tables, and the heat pushed her back.

Colt reported the fire to Sara and requested assistance.

But Jordyn knew fire trucks would have a hard time getting to them through the storm. "The BoneDigger is destroying evidence. We have to put out the flames." She ran back into the hall and pointed. "Nick, grab the extinguisher. Quick!"

The man obeyed and returned with Eve at his heels. Nick dispersed the liquid.

Moments later, they had the flames under control.

"Nick and Eve, check the rest of the remains," Jordyn said.

Her team inspected the evidence and quickly confirmed everything was intact, despite the suspect's attempt to destroy the evidence.

They had arrived just in time.

Thanks to Bones.

His alert had not only saved them but also the skeletons the BoneDigger obviously wanted to destroy.

Jordyn grasped the edge of the table to steady her weakened legs as her heartbeat accelerated. They had to stop this madman before he took more lives. Morgan's face flashed in her mind. Was she still alive? Why hadn't the constabulary found her? It was as if she'd vanished… Just like Lincoln.

The smoke remained heavy in the small room, stealing her air. Jordyn held her hand over her mouth.

Eve coughed.

Nick guided Eve toward the door. "Time to get you out of here. We all have to leave."

Her team stepped into the hall.

Sara's voice boomed through Colt's radio. "Peters, watch your back."

He hit the talk button. "Fire is out in the lab. Are there others?"

"Not that we can see. We feel it's a ruse to get you out of the building. The premier's men are canvassing every room." A crash sounded in the background.

"What's happening, Greer?" Colt asked.

"Hurricane took out another window. Lots of damage. Gotta go help."

"Copy that." Colt hooked the radio back onto his shoulder before approaching Jordyn. "You ran off without protection. Stop taking risks. A madman is out to get you, or did you forget that?"

Colt's tone revealed he wasn't happy with her actions. His anger turned his normally soft expression into one of contempt.

"I haven't, Colt, but—" She pointed to the

bones on the closest table. "I believe these are Lincoln's remains." She hesitated, contemplating whether she should say the thought poised on her tongue. "I had to protect them. For you. For your family."

He hung his head. "I'm sorry. You scared me, and I don't want to lose you." His gaze met hers. "Again."

What does that *mean?*

She analyzed his green eyes in the dim lighting. She let out a small cry before she could stifle her reaction to whatever emotion shone through his intense look.

Hope? Longing?

His eyes veered to her lips.

Was he thinking of kissing her? Now? Here in a smoky room?

Bones moved in between them and nudged Jordyn, breaking the moment.

Colt cleared his throat and rubbed the dog's fur. "Good boy. Yes, we need to get away from the smoke. Time to—"

Eve's scream pierced the early-morning hours.

Bones barked.

Colt raised his weapon and edged out of the room.

Lord, help Eve to be okay. Jordyn scrambled into the hallway.

And halted.

A man wearing a balaclava and dressed in a

maintenance uniform had Eve in a steady hold with a gun jammed into her temple.

Nick was nowhere to be seen.

What had happened in such a short time frame?

"I warned you." The man's raspy whisper concealed his voice. He waggled the gun at Colt. "Drop your weapon, Constable." He placed the barrel back on Eve's temple. "Or she dies."

"Take it easy, man." Colt lowered his Sig and placed it on the floor.

Jordyn raised her hands, stepping forward. Tangled emotions churned her stomach, threatening to immobilize her.

"Stay behind me," Colt ordered.

She couldn't. Eve was not only a colleague but also a friend, and Jordyn wanted information about Morgan. "Take me, and tell me where you have my sister."

He tilted his head. "Your sister?"

She dug her nails into her palms, curbing the anger bubbling inside her. *Stay calm. Eve is depending on you.* She took another step. "Don't play dumb. I know you're the BoneDigger. Who's your accomplice? The woman with the blond ponytail?"

His dark eyes widened.

She'd caught him off guard.

Colt tugged on her arm. "Don't antagonize him, Jordyn."

"I have to save her." She had promised herself

she'd do anything to keep those she loved safe—including risking her own life.

"You can do that by giving me the bones you dug up." The gunman's garbled voice grew louder. "They're my property."

His what? He believed he owned the remains of those he'd killed? How sick was this man?

"Never. That's evidence." Jordyn sensed Colt's movements beside her as Bones growled.

"You just signed all your death warrants." The gunman shifted the weapon in Jordyn's direction.

"No!" Colt yelled, rushing forward.

Bones barked as a shot rang out.

Jordyn's heartbeat thundered in her ears as Bones tackled her to the ground, protecting her from the masked assailant's bullet.

The gun clattered to the tile floor.

Sounds of a scuffle followed.

Colt and the man were in a crocodile roll, fighting for the discarded weapon.

Thankfully, Eve had scrambled away and was cowering against the wall.

Jordyn had to save Colt, and she would use the one weapon the BoneDigger had underestimated.

"Bones, get 'em!" she commanded, pointing toward the duo. When she and Colt had been together, he'd trained Bones to obey Jordyn's commands. Just in case.

Now was the time.

The K-9 leaped off her, raced to his partner's side and bit down hard on the suspect's arm.

The BoneDigger yelled and scrambled backward.

A shot rang out, and a female in a balaclava appeared around the corner, catching them all off guard.

The BoneDigger took the distraction as an opportunity and pushed Bones off him before scrambling to his feet. He clutched his arm, and the pair bolted through a nearby exit.

"Colt!" Jordyn hurried to his side.

"I'm okay." He sat up and grabbed his radio. "Greer, two suspects just attacked us. One male, one female. Heading down the northeast stairwell from the second floor."

Anxious words sailed through the airwaves. "We'll try to intercept them. You guys okay?"

"We're good." Colt pushed himself up. "Where's Nick?" he asked Jordyn.

"I'm here." Nick appeared around the corner, Vance Chambers at his side.

Doubt niggled at Jordyn, locking her neck muscles into a tight knot. Why had Nick abandoned the team in their hour of need?

Colt noted the twisted expression on Jordyn's face. He could almost read her mind. Where had Nick disappeared to? Why had he left Eve alone?

None of it made any sense. "Nick, where did you go?"

"To the other end of the floor for a quick second, and I found Dr. Chambers in the stairwell." Nick's eyes narrowed. "Why?"

Colt buried his rising anger at the man before him. "You left Eve unattended, and the BoneDigger attacked her."

His jaw dropped. "What?"

Colt inspected the man's face for deception but found none. He turned his attention to the ME. "Where did you come from?"

Dr. Chambers pinched his lips into a flat line before responding. "I don't report to you—but if you must know, I stayed here overnight to work on my backlog of paperwork. I couldn't leave anyway with the hurricane raging outside. I heard the fire alarm and wanted to make sure everything was okay in Autopsy."

Why didn't Colt believe either of these men? He had to get the others to safety, then he would grill the duo later. "Everyone, return to the lab. The breeze from the broken window should have helped clear the smoke by now."

Nick, Eve and Dr. Chambers hurried down the hall.

Colt drew Jordyn aside. "Jordyn, how well do you know Nick?"

"You don't believe him and you're wondering where he went. Me too." She bit her lip. "The chief ME recommended Nick, and he's been with me for a couple of years now. I can't imagine he'd be dangerous."

"Agreed, but I want to ask him and Dr. Chambers more questions. He seemed to appear out of nowhere." Colt scratched his head. He surmised the BoneDigger had pulled the alarm to bring them out into the open so he could attack. He'd set the fire to destroy evidence and stop the medical examiner from identifying his victims, which proved that something in their identification would lead to him.

Colt had to keep not only Jordyn and her team safe but also the bones. They were the key to resolving this case.

An object by the lab's door caught his attention. "What's that?" He pointed and unsnapped his flashlight for a better look in the dim corridor. He pointed the beam at the item.

Another lynx carving.

Had the BoneDigger dropped it in his race to get out of the room after he'd set the fire?

And more importantly, was it meant for one of them?

Jordyn drew in a sharp breath. "Who was he planning this carving for? You don't think—"

He knew what she was thinking. "Let's not go there, okay?" Colt hustled into the lab and placed it on the table, then peered through a magnifying glass. "Well, I'll be."

"What? Let me see," Jordyn said.

He stepped aside.

Eve and Nick joined them at the table. Dr. Chambers stood by the window.

Jordyn inspected the carving, then popped her head up, eyes wide. "Why is this one different?"

The carving had a partial verse engraved on it: *For the wages of sin is death...*

"No idea. And why not the entire verse from Romans?" Colt asked.

Eve leaned closer to the carving. "What does the verse say?"

"'For the wages of sin is death; but the gift of God is eternal life through Jesus Christ our Lord,'" Colt and Jordyn said, quoting it together.

Dr. Chambers approached. "So why leave the rest of the verse off the carving?"

"Because he's playing God and chooses who dies." Colt placed the carving beside the others.

"Plus, we dug up his graveyard, and he didn't like it," Jordyn said.

Colt nodded at her assessment. "He tried to destroy the bones because he doesn't want the remains identified. Something in their identities links them back to him."

Eve examined the wood carvings. "Maybe a friend, relative or something?"

"Let's stop guessing. Facts, people, facts." Jordyn yanked a sweater from off the back of a chair and put it on. "It's freezing in here. We need the window fixed."

"Sorry, the makeshift covering isn't holding very well," Nick said, glancing through a different window. "Wait, there are lights in the distance. It looks like the storm has subsided somewhat."

The electricity flipped on as if in response, flooding the room with much-needed light.

"Hallelujah." Jordyn scooted off her chair. "Time to get to work."

Colt checked his phone. "It's still early. You need more rest, Jordyn."

"I'm wide-awake now, but I could use some coffee. Do we have a drug-free grind?" She chuckled.

"Yes, I made a pot last night using my Columbian beans," Nick said. "And I'm fine. I'll make you some."

Perfect. Colt would take this opportunity to talk to the man alone. "I'll come with you. After, I'd like to take a close look at the photos you took at the crime scene."

"Eve, can you project them onto the screen? I want to continue with the next set of bones." Jordyn got to work on examining the skeleton.

"You got it, boss." Eve sat at the computer.

Colt addressed Bones, "Stay."

His partner obeyed.

Colt joined Nick in the lunchroom. "Can we talk?"

Nick added coffee beans into the grinder. "Don't like the sound of that. What's up?"

"I suspect you're holding something back, based on your response to where you were earlier."

Nick turned the grinder on and mumbled, his words lost in the noise.

Was he avoiding the question or plotting an answer?

"Sorry, didn't catch that." Colt spoke aloud and dropped down onto a stool at the kitchen island.

"Just don't appreciate your insinuation." Nick poured the grounds into a filter, then placed it in the coffee maker.

Colt raised his hands. "Only doing my job. I'm here to protect Jordyn and now her team. That's you. I can't do that if you're hiding something."

After filling the water reservoir, Nick placed the carafe on the burner and turned on the machine. "Look, I heard a noise and ran to check."

"But you didn't hear Eve's scream?" Colt crossed his arms. "Do you understand why I'm confused?" He didn't mean to sound sarcastic, but he couldn't help himself.

Nick slammed his hand on the counter. "Okay. It was farther than just down the hall. I went up a level to get these." He pulled a pack of cigarettes from his pocket.

Colt exhaled, relief relaxing his muscles. "That's all? Why not say that before?"

"Because Jordyn was the one who helped me quit, and I didn't want to admit that my nerves from everything that's happening fueled my craving. And I needed a fix." He opened the garbage and tossed the cigarettes inside. "I respect Jordyn a great deal and didn't want her to be disappointed in me."

"Understood. So that's all?"

He raised his hand. "Scout's honor. I promise."

"Good." Another question entered Colt's mind. "Where did you run across Dr. Chambers?"

"I was coming back down and met him by the entrance to our floor. Gotta say, he looked surprised to see me and was out of breath from running."

"Maybe he ran down the stairs in front of you. Isn't his office on the floor one level up?" Colt snatched a mug off the rack on the counter.

"No, I heard someone below me, and it had to have been him." Nick poured himself a cup.

Perhaps Dr. Chambers was keeping a secret from his coworkers. "Thanks for letting me know. Let's grab some caffeine and check out the photos. I'd like your opinion on them."

Colt sipped the dark-roasted coffee fifteen minutes later, studying the pictures Eve had displayed on the screen. Dr. Chambers had mysteriously left the lab, claiming he wasn't feeling well and required rest.

For now, Colt would let it go. He turned to Nick. "Thoughts?"

The man tapped his chin, then leaned closer. "We have five graves dug near trees, but check this out." He clicked on the computer, arranging the photos side by side. "What do you see?"

Colt inspected each image, taking his time. "Wait, he skipped this tree." He pointed. "Why?"

"Just a sec." Nick tapped on his tablet and casted the photos onto their whiteboard. He picked up a marker and drew a connecting line to each grave. "Catch it now?"

"A perfect circle." Colt held up one picture. "And the tree he ignored would have broken the circle."

"Exactly. I just don't understand why."

"Good eye." Colt was impressed with Nick's deductive skills.

Jordyn approached them. "What if the circle represents some type of ritual?"

"Like a religious one?" Colt asked.

"Or a university hazing." Nick snapped his fingers. "I'm going to search for that. Hopefully, our internet came back with the power." He clicked on the keyboard.

Jordyn eyed the photos. "I feel like we're close yet far away in solving this unmarked-grave mystery."

"How much longer before you send everything to Dr. Chambers?" Colt asked.

"We still have more work to do, so it will probably be another couple of weeks. It takes time, and we need to do this correctly. Hopefully, the BoneDigger leaves us alone." She moved over to the window, Bones at her feet. "It finally looks like the storm has passed. Maybe a sign of good things to come."

Colt suppressed a sigh. Did she really believe that?

Somehow he doubted the BoneDigger would take a break and let her finish her job.

Not if he was tied to any of the victims.

Nope. He wouldn't risk his identity being exposed.

Especially if he had more targets in mind.

ELEVEN

Jordyn sipped her coffee as she stared out the window at her parents' cottage residence two and a half weeks later. She had finished her documentation in record time, and now Dr. Chambers, with the help of a group of medical examiners, would carefully review everything to determine how each victim had died. She had sent her findings in stages, hoping it would speed up the ME's process.

Hurricane Jezebel had finally passed through their region, damaging most of the Charock Harbour community. Cleanup crews worked around the clock to clear the area and make repairs. She hadn't minded, as it allowed her to give her team time off. Meanwhile, she had set up a makeshift office in the cottage's dining room.

Unfortunately, there had been no further word on Morgan's whereabouts. Even though Jordyn hadn't recently spoken much to her sister, she longed to hear Morgan's voice. She had to share the fact that she'd forgiven her and wanted back in her life. Not that Jordyn expected an instant reconnection, but it would be a start.

She scanned the horizon for some hope of a break in the dreary sky. It was late afternoon, but dusk had once again descended. Even though the storm had passed, the sun refused to shine.

"Morgie, where are you?" Jordyn failed to even consider what Ursula Baine had speculated on the news—that Morgan had probably been killed and the police hadn't found her remains. Jordyn pursed her lips. "That's not true. It can't be." A tear escaped, and she wiped it away.

Woof!

Jordyn squatted in front of the German shepherd and checked behind her to ensure Colt was nowhere in sight. Bones was working, but she wanted to show him how much she enjoyed being around her canine friend. Assured of his partner's absence, she kissed the dog's face.

He licked hers in response.

She rubbed behind his ears. "It will be our little secret, okay, bud?"

He barked.

"What secret?" Colt asked, skulking up behind her.

She jumped. "Nothing. What's going on?"

"Just got word Ursula will be giving another report shortly." Colt pointed at Bones. "Why does my dog have lipstick on his head?"

Busted.

"No idea. Let's go watch our *favorite* reporter." She spun on her heels and hustled into the living room, suppressing her laughter over her and Bones's secret.

Jordyn picked up the remote and sunk into a chair.

"It's gonna be okay." Colt placed a hand on her shoulder.

She startled. "Is it? We can't outrun the BoneDigger or find my sister."

"I've been praying. God's got this." Colt paused. "Sorry, it's not what you wanted to hear. I hate when people give me pat answers, and I just did the very thing I despise."

The familiar tones of breaking-news music blared on the news station, stalling their conversation. Ursula appeared on the screen, sitting beside the station's news anchor.

"We interrupt your regular programming to give you an update on the BoneDigger case." The man tapped his papers on the surface and turned to Ursula. "Tell us what you've uncovered."

She smiled into the camera. "Channel 5 News has discovered that police found lynx carvings in all the BoneDigger's graves..."

What? Jordyn stole a glance at Colt.

His mouth hung open.

He was just as surprised by Ursula's statement as she was.

The lynx carvings were not public knowledge, so how had the reporter gotten the information?

Ursula's newscast went on to say how there were no further leads in the disappearance of Morgan Crandall, but she urged the community to come forward with any information.

Jordyn turned off the television. "How did she know about the carvings, Colt?"

"Would Nick or Eve tell her?" he asked.

"Never. I trust them explicitly. It has to be someone else."

"But who?"

Jordyn shuffled into the kitchen after changing into comfy jammies and a housecoat later that evening. She put on the kettle to enjoy a chamomile tea before bed.

Bones rubbed against her legs, reminding her of his presence. The dog had continued to stick by her side, taking his protective duty seriously.

Jordyn would miss him once this dreadful situation ended. During supper that evening, the Millers had discussed the case briefly. Jordyn had fought her emotions when her mother broke down after Colt had mentioned they still didn't have any leads on Morgan's whereabouts. Somehow, the BoneDigger had hidden her sister well.

Her father had given his wife a sedative to help her rest.

Jordyn stared at the ceiling. "Lord, Mom puts

her trust in You. Please find Morgan alive." She squeezed her eyes shut as a tear trickled down her cheek.

"Amen," Colt said.

She startled at his voice and turned. "Don't sneak up on me like that."

"Sorry. You wanna talk about it?"

"I don't understand why God allows so much darkness in the world." Jordyn plunked a tea bag into a mug.

"Honestly, I don't know the answer." He grabbed a cup from the rack beside the coffee maker. "I just choose to believe He's in control."

"I'm not so sure about that any longer." She plucked a cookie from a container. "How can you when He took Lincoln from you?"

"I struggle with the guilt every day, Jordyn, but I refuse to believe God has abandoned me." He took a tea bag and dropped it into his cup. "Don't get me wrong—at times, I feel like I'm slipping into a dark place. But then God gives me some type of encouragement."

"What do you mean?"

"Something like an uplifting note from a friend or a phone call from my pastor saying he's praying for me."

The teakettle whistled, and Jordyn removed it from the burner, then poured the hot water into their mugs. "I want to trust He's near, but I can't see through the darkness."

"He's there, Jordyn." Colt placed his hand on her arm. "But it's okay to wonder. Remember, even His disciples doubted. Thomas had to feel the holes in Jesus's hands to believe."

Jordyn dunked her tea bag a few times to hasten the steeping process. "I miss our conversations."

"Me too," Colt whispered.

He did?

She studied his intense expression. "Then why did you leave?"

He moved a strand of hair behind her ear, letting his fingers linger on her cheek. "I wish—"

"There you two are." Her father strode into the kitchen.

Colt dropped his hand.

Jordyn sipped her tea, concealing her sorrow. His presence over the past two weeks had brought them closer once again, and only added to her desire of wanting Colt back in her life, but it would never happen.

"Colt, can I speak to my daughter alone?"

"Of course." Colt turned to Jordyn. "See you in the morning."

She nodded, words failing to form without the risk of spilling tears.

"Bones, guard." Colt picked up his mug. "He'll stay by your bed. 'Night." He left the room.

"Jordyn, have a seat." Her father poured himself a coffee and took it to the table.

She took a chair opposite him. "What's up, Dad?"

"I'm concerned you're working yourself too hard."

She bit her lip to stifle the words she wanted to say. When would he ever tell her he was proud of her accomplishments? "Dad, my work is important. I help law enforcement. Don't you want these victims' families to have closure?"

He slammed his hand on the table. "I want both of my daughters to be safe."

Bones barked.

"Dad, calm down." She patted Bones's head. "It's okay, bud. Just Mr. Grumpy Pants here."

Her father slouched in his chair, crossing his arms. "I'm sorry. I want them to find Morgan… alive."

"Colt's station is doing everything they can to find her." Jordyn took another sip of her tea as an idea formed. Her relationship with her father would never change until they built a bridge to close the gap between them. "Dad, I need to ask you something—and please be honest with me."

Her father unfolded his arms and leaned forward. "What?"

"I know you said previously this was nothing, but I keep having a recurring nightmare about a car accident from when I was little. You're driving and we hit something before the car skids. I hear myself scream and then I wake up. I can't help but feel it's a suppressed memory."

He averted his eyes as he sipped his coffee. "It's only a dream, Jordyn."

Why didn't she believe him?

"What aren't you telling me, Dad? Did something happen when I was about five?"

He jerked upright, his hip bumping the table.

Jordyn's mug crashed to the tile floor, shattering into pieces. A symbol of their broken relationship?

His actions proved to Jordyn he was withholding something from the past that inhibited their future.

Until he told the truth, she couldn't trust her own father.

"Still nothing?" Colt struggled to keep the frustration from his voice after Sergeant Warren informed him the next morning there were no recent developments on their search for Morgan. It had been too long since her abduction, and his boss had lost all hope that the premier's daughter was still alive. Since the BoneDigger's text to Colt indicated he was aware he'd kidnapped the wrong twin, Russell Miller had released a statement regarding his daughter's abduction along with the constabulary. He'd sent out a heart-wrenching plea to the public before offering a reward for her safe return. However, no new leads had materialized since.

"Afraid not, but the phones have been ringing off the hook. Most are prank calls, looking for the reward money."

"Figures." Colt sipped his black coffee before continuing, "We're laying low for now. Jordyn gave her staff a much-needed break. We're hoping to hear information from Dr. Chambers on the remains soon."

"Forensics didn't find any fingerprints on the wood carvings, so that's a dead end."

"No surprise there. Anything you want me to do from here?" Colt and Bones were still staying at the premier's residence, Jordyn's protection was their number one priority. She had closed her lab for a few days and canceled classes.

"Just keep Jordyn safe. Don't let her go anywhere alone. The BoneDigger has been too silent. I don't understand why this serial killer seems to have stopped killing, or maybe he hasn't, and we just haven't found his graves."

Colt had wondered the same thing. "Could be. Perhaps he just went on with his life. No idea. I don't claim to understand a killer's mind."

The sergeant huffed. "Makes me nervous he'll strike again, at any time, and I don't need Premier Russell on my back for another missing daughter."

"Roger that. Call me with any further updates."

"Absolutely." His sergeant ended the call.

Bones's claws clicked on the hardwood floors as he and Jordyn entered the spacious living room.

Jordyn was ending a call on her cell phone. "Okay, thanks, Vance. Advise me when you learn more about the others." She clicked off and sat down in the rocker beside him. "I have news."

Her eyes softened as she bit her lip.

He pocketed his cell phone and strangled the armrests until his knuckles turned white.

She peeled his fingers from the chair and took his hands in hers. "Vance received the dental records and confirmed the identity. It is Lincoln—and he was shot, as I suspected." She rubbed the back of his hand with her thumb. "I'm so sorry."

Heaviness tightened his chest at the news of his brother's murder. Time suspended, and the fight with his brother reentered his mind, fresh and vivid. What could he have done differently that day? The question had plagued him for ten years. Regret knotted his stomach as tears blanketed his vision, blurring Jordyn's beautiful face. "I knew it. I failed him. Failed my parents." He hated to show his emotions, but he couldn't stop them this time. "I'm sorry for crying. I'm not normally like this."

Jordyn brought him into an embrace. "Let it out, Colt. Heroes need comforting, too, you know."

Hero? He was no hero. He'd abandoned his only brother. All Colt's insecurities gushed out in front of the woman he had also failed. His failures had forced him to let the love of his life go. *God, help me. I need to feel Your arms around me too. Or have I also failed You?*

Jordyn hugged him tighter, as if she could read his thoughts, and he wanted to stay nestled in her arms, never letting go.

But then he remembered her love for children and his vow not to have any. He pushed away from her.

Was that disappointment shining in her eyes?

Great, you did it again—failed someone you love.

And yes, he still loved Dr. Jordyn Miller. In this moment, he realized he'd never stopped. But once again, he had to relinquish her. She deserved more than him.

Bones nudged Colt's leg before placing his head on his lap, whining.

The dog had sensed his partner's shift in mood.

Colt rubbed Bones's head. "I'll be okay, bud."

"He loves you." Jordyn ruffled his ears.

Bones barked in agreement.

A smile tugged at Colt's lips. Nothing like his best friend to help lighten the mood.

Colt willed strength into his legs and pushed himself to his feet. "I need to tell my parents. Now. Before this news becomes public."

"Understood. I'll go with you."

"I hate to involve you, but I also can't leave you unguarded."

She touched his arm. "It's okay. I want to go."

"Thank you."

After speaking to his father and ensuring his parents were both at home, Colt drove into their subdivision on the edge of Charock Harbour.

Clouds still blanketed the region, along with mist and a dense fog, sending chills throughout his body. He put the car in Park in his parents' driveway and cut the engine. For a moment, he sat there, a question echoing in his mind.

How would they take the news that their son had been murdered?

Jordyn unbuckled her seat belt. "They need to know the truth, Colt."

"How do you do that?" he asked.

"Do what?"

"Read my mind. I can't help wondering how they'll react. Confirmation of his death is bad enough, but murder? It will crush my mom." He exhaled. "Now she'll never forgive me for abandoning her son that day."

"She's tougher than you give her credit for."

"I hope so." He opened his door. "Time to get this done."

Colt, Jordyn and Bones exited the vehicle and trudged up the stone walkway.

Colt rang the bell before opening the door. It

had been his childhood home, but he wanted to alert them to their presence.

He entered the foyer, and music stopped him in his tracks.

A recording of Linc playing guitar years ago blasted through the house.

It was as if his mother had somehow known why Colt was coming.

The music was silenced, and moments later, his father appeared around the corner. "We're in the living room." His face looked grim. "Is it Linc?"

Colt nodded and shoved his pending emotions aside, steeling his shoulders. "Please pray for Mom because there's more."

Tears glistened in his father's eyes. "She figured something happened, and that's why she wanted to listen to Linc's music." He peeked around Colt. "Hi, Jordyn. Good to see you."

"You too. I'm just sorry it's under these conditions." Jordyn unzipped her coat.

Colt gestured them forward. "Let's go. Bones, release." He knew his mother would need the dog's comfort.

They moved into the living room.

Bones bounded toward Colt's mother, who was knitting in her rocker beside a roaring fire in the stone hearth.

She dropped her needles and held her arms open. "Bones. You came." She hugged the German shepherd.

Colt sighed inwardly. *Why can't you react like that when I visit, Mom?* And now, with the news he was about to tell her, she'd never forgive him. "Hi, Mom."

She turned her attention from Bones to her son, then to Jordyn. "Hello, Jordyn."

Still no greeting for him.

Jordyn made her way over to his mother. "Abigail, so good to see you again."

His mother stood and pulled Jordyn into a bear hug. "I've missed you."

"I'm sorry I haven't been over to see you." Jordyn squeezed his mother's shoulder, then stepped aside and took a seat on the sofa.

"Abby, Colt is here, too, you know," his father said.

Colt hugged his mother. His arms smothered her slight frame, and he stiffened at her protruding rib cage. "Mom, haven't you been eating?"

She tensed at his touch but remained silent.

He guided her back into the rocker and squatted in front of her. "Mom, I have news."

She chewed on her lip, staring at the floor.

"You've probably heard about the unmarked graves we found on the outskirts of town." He let his statement sink in for a moment. "Some of those remains belong to Linc, Mom. He's gone. I'm so sorry." A tear slipped down his face.

Her eyes widened, snapping upward to meet

Colt's. Then she did the one thing Colt had never expected.

She smiled and wiped away Colt's tear, letting her fingers linger on his face. "He's with Jesus."

Colt's father kneeled on the other side of Colt, providing a unified front. He put a hand on his wife's arm. "We finally know. Now we can rest."

She turned her face to her husband. "Yes. We have to make funeral arrangements."

His mother had refused to give Linc a celebration of life without knowing what had happened.

Colt took her hand, guessing that what he was about to say would probably push his mother back into silence. He took a deep breath. "There's more." He addressed his father. "Someone killed Linc that night."

His father bolted upright. "What? How? Was it this BoneDigger I keep hearing about?"

"I can answer that," Jordyn said. "The ME confirmed he died from a gunshot wound."

Colt noted she'd left out where the BoneDigger had shot Linc. His mother didn't need to know that information. "Mom, I know you've been extremely upset with me for the past ten years. This is all my fault." He rested his head on her lap. "Can you ever forgive me? I miss you."

"Dennis and Jordyn, can you give us the room, please?" She paused. "I need to talk to my son."

Colt lifted his head.

His father and Jordyn nodded. Before she left

the room, Jordyn stopped in the doorway and turned. “Bones, come.”

The dog obeyed her command.

His mother stood and moved to the couch, patting the seat beside her. “Come sit.”

A surge of dread passed over him, threatening to overpower his emotions in anticipation of whatever she was about to say.

He nestled himself next to his frail mother.

She poked him in the chest. “First, this is not your fault. Lincoln was a big boy and had a hand in your fight. Second, I never blamed you, and I’m sorry I let you believe that for ten years. I’m a terrible mother.”

Those were not the words he’d expected to come out of her mouth. “But why haven’t you spoken to me, Mom? I needed you.”

She caressed his face. “Because I didn’t want to lose you too. I was scared to get close to you for fear of having to say goodbye to another son, so I did the best thing I could think of—I withdrew into a shell.”

“That makes no sense.”

“My grieving heart held me captive. Until now.”

“You needed closure.” Colt took his mother’s hand. “You may not blame me, but I can’t get rid of the guilt. I should never have left him on the side of the road.”

“How could you have known? We didn’t even

lock our doors back then, so why would we think something this sinister would happen?" She patted the back of his hand. "Can *you* forgive *me* for shutting you out?"

He searched her face. Could he? He had to, if he wanted her back in his life. And he did. "Yes, Mom. I love you so much."

"I love you too." She kissed his cheek, then hugged him. "Now, you need to forgive yourself, son. It's what God wants of you."

Colt doubted he could ever carry out her difficult command.

TWELVE

Jordyn's cell phone buzzed, waking her from the recurring nightmare that had been plaguing her dreams. She grabbed the device, checked the caller and time. Why was Constable Lavigne phoning her at two in the morning? She swallowed to clear her throat and hit Accept. "Dr. Miller here."

"Sorry for waking you, but I just received a call about another skeleton," Harley said. "Thought you'd want to meet me there."

She lurched into a seated position on the bed, disturbing Bones, who was lying at her feet. "What? Where?"

"Caller said it was farther into the forest under another balsam fir."

Jordyn threw off the comforter and swung her legs over the side, slipping into her plaid slippers. "How did Greta miss that?" Their GPR device normally caught everything.

Bones stretched and jumped to the floor.

"I'm guessing we didn't go that far into the woods. Plus, we were trying to outrun a hurricane."

"True, or it could have been the rocky terrain." Jordyn pulled out a clean pair of cargo pants and a shirt from a dresser drawer. "Who called it in?"

"Kalvin Anderson, the night guard at Charock Lighting."

"Have you contacted Colt?"

"Yes, he's—"

A quiet knock sounded.

"Never mind. He's here. I won't call in my team yet, but I'll do a preliminary check. Kind of hard in the dark, though."

"I know it's the middle of the night, but I was concerned an animal might drag the remains away or something before you had a look."

"Understood. We'll meet you there as soon as we can." She clicked off. "Coming, Colt."

After picking up a limited amount of equipment from her lab on the way, Jordyn, Colt and Bones arrived at the cemetery forty minutes later. Colt parked beside Harley Lavigne.

They exited their vehicle and approached the constable.

Jordyn secured her protective hood. "Where's the guard?"

"Not sure. Just got here too."

"Wait, you haven't processed the scene?" Colt asked.

"No, roads were blocked, and I had to take a detour." He gestured toward the warehouse. "Let's find Mr. Anderson."

Jordyn trudged behind Colt and Harley with Bones by her side. She extracted a flashlight from her shoulder bag and scanned the cemetery beside the building. Multiple monuments marked the graves, put there by loved ones paying homage to those they'd lost. Wilted flowers rested in bronze vases in front of some tombstones. Blackened, worn stones revealed the years they'd been in the cemetery.

She rested the beam on a mound in front of one tombstone. "Wait, what's that?"

Colt stopped. "Looks like a body." He rested his hand on his weapon and veered toward the gravesite.

Harley did the same.

Jordyn approached with caution, thankful Bones was at her side.

"Sir, are you all right?" Colt asked.

Silence.

"Sir, can you hear me?" Colt advanced closer and turned. "It's the security guard." He squatted and placed two fingers on the man's neck. "He's alive."

Harley kneeled and nudged Kalvin's shoulder. "Mr. Anderson, can you hear us?"

Kalvin stirred and groaned. "What—what happened?"

Colt helped him sit. "You called us, stating you found another unmarked grave. What happened after that?"

Jordyn scanned the dark cemetery and shivered, not from the cold but from the foreboding flood of unrest settling into her bones. What had occurred in this tiny graveyard and its surrounding area? Had the BoneDigger struck again?

Chills slithered down her spine, wreaking havoc on her already frayed nerves.

"Wait, I remember." Kalvin's voice boomed over the stillness. "I came out for a smoke and took a walk in the forest."

"In the middle of the night?" Harley asked.

"The stillness soothes me, and I needed some fresh air." Kalvin massaged his right temple. "That's when I found a hole that an animal had dug up. I looked closer and saw a skeleton."

"Then what happened?" Colt helped the man stand.

"I walked back here and called you guys. Better reception." He scratched his head. "Wait, after I called 911, something pricked my neck—then I don't remember anything until you nudged me."

Jordyn approached. "Can I see?"

Kalvin unzipped his jacket and opened the neckline.

Jordyn shined her light and pointed. "See that red mark? I think he was drugged."

"Mr. Anderson, we need to get you to the hospital to get checked out," Colt said. "They'll take a blood sample."

Kalvin swayed. "No! No hospitals."

"Why, Mr. Anderson?" Harley helped steady the man.

His eyes narrowed. "Terrible experience. Besides, I'm fine. Feeling better already."

"How about we get a paramedic to check you out and take some blood?" Colt asked.

"They can do that?" He chewed on his lip.

Colt dug his cell phone out of his pocket. "Some can. We'll advise them of the situation and ask for a paramedic with the correct level of care."

Jordyn placed her hand on Colt's arm. "Just a sec." She turned to face Kalvin. "Are you strong enough to show us where you found the grave? I need to examine it as soon as possible."

"I think so." He gestured toward the woods. "This way." He fumbled for his flashlight and turned it on.

They followed him to the edge of the cemetery and entered the forest.

Jordyn shined her light on the ground, watching for stumps and protruding rocks in the rugged terrain.

Moments later, Kalvin stopped close to a tree and directed his beam at a section of disturbed soil under the fir. "Right there."

"Okay, thanks. Please step back." Jordyn retrieved her sketch pad. "Constable Lavigne, can you take Mr. Anderson back the way we came?"

"Got it. We can't contaminate the scene. I'll call for a paramedic to check him out." He led the guard out of the forest.

Jordyn drew a rough sketch to map out the scene before inspecting the remains. The skeleton's lower portion was exposed, while the soil still hid the upper torso and skull. Bones of a foot sat beside the grave. She hauled out her camera and took several pictures using the flash. "I need daylight," she told Colt. "It's too hard to see anything. I'll call Eve and Nick in the morning and ask them to bring our equipment." She pushed herself up. "Can you get constables to protect the area for now, until we can come back in the daylight?"

"Of course. I'll call it in." He clicked on his radio and requested assistance.

Jordyn removed pin flags from her gear. "For now, let's set up a perimeter." She handed Colt a few flags. "Stick them all around the site."

Together, they set a wide border to mark the grave. Then Jordyn returned to the skeleton. "I can't believe we missed this one. Could someone have just buried it?"

"Seems unlikely." He pointed to the foot bones. "I'm guessing an animal dug it up."

"But that doesn't explain why we didn't find it earlier." She shined her light around. "I'm sure

Nick sent Greta this far into the forest. Must have been the rugged terrain."

"It's odd." Colt bent to plant his last flag into the ground.

Bones barked and pranced around Jordyn, clearly agitated.

"Colt? What's wrong with Bones?"

He turned. "Bones, heel."

The dog continued to circle Jordyn, barking and growling.

He was protecting her—but from what?

Colt shined his flashlight beam into the trees. "Hold still."

"What is it?" Jordyn froze at Colt's forceful tone.

He gestured to their right. "A litter of lynxes just surrounded us."

Multiple pairs of eyes shone between the firs, followed by high-pitched yowls.

Terror seized Jordyn's limbs, immobilizing her. She held her breath.

Had the lynxes come back to the unmarked grave to claim their territory?

Colt unholstered his Sig with caution, not wanting to send the animals into a frenzy. Lynxes weren't known for attacking humans, but he wouldn't take that chance. Bones continued to bark, circling Jordyn. He was protecting her—not from the BoneDigger but from a different kind of predator. "Jordyn, don't run. That will provoke them. I'm going to shoot into the air to scare them away. After I do, slowly back up and talk loudly. That will help tell them who's boss." First he had to warn Lavigne so he wouldn't come running. Colt pressed his radio button. "Lavigne, we're surrounded by lynxes. Be warned. Going to shoot into the air."

"Copy that," Lavigne replied seconds later. "Go ahead."

Colt shot three rounds into the air. "Yell and wave your arms," he told Jordyn. Then he turned to his partner. "Bones, speak!" On command, the K-9 barked.

Jordyn and Colt made lots of noise while Bones barked louder.

The lynxes hissed before retreating deeper into the wilderness.

Colt let out a long breath. "That was close. You okay?" He shined the light toward Jordyn.

Her widened eyes glistened in the beam. "I will be when we get inside your SUV. Another reason to come back in the daylight."

"Agreed. You need anything else from the scene?"

"I'm good. Let's go before they come back. You'll have to warn the constables who'll be guarding the site." She rubbed her eyes. "I need a few more hours' sleep. Can we head back to Dad's before I get the team here at daybreak?"

"Absolutely."

After updating the constables and ensuring Kalvin was okay, Colt drove onto the highway.

"That was an interesting outing." Jordyn took out her cell phone. "I'm going to text the team and get them to meet me in the morning." Her phone glowed in the dim interior as she tapped out her message.

He chuckled. "Wouldn't exactly call it an *outing.* Glad we could secure everything. Lavigne has requested other constables sweep the area for anything suspicious. We still don't know what or who dug up the skeleton."

Colt swerved around a hole in the road.

A thud sounded beside him.

"Shoot. I dropped my phone," Jordyn said. "Can you turn the light on for a sec?" She leaned forward, feeling around the floorboard. "Is it possible someone moved the remains here just today, and the lynxes scared them off before they could finish burying the bones?"

He hit the light button. "Well, anything's possible." Colt eased up on the accelerator, anticipating the sharp curve in the road ahead. The twisty highway hugged the ocean and was dangerous in spots, especially in the dark.

"Maybe the BoneDigger missed a grave."

"I'm not so sure." Colt stole a glance at Jordyn. She had taken off her personal protective suit and hoodie; her hair was disheveled, poking up in various directions. Even in the middle of the night, with no makeup and messy hair, she was still beautiful. He flipped on the radio to distract himself from the rising feelings he'd hoped were buried.

She puffed out a sigh. "I'm confused. These kills weren't recent. Don't most serial killers keep murdering?"

"Not always. The sergeant and I were talking about that earlier. Some stop after they get married or have children. But something definitely interrupted his killing spree."

"But now that we've unearthed his gravesites, will he start again? Will he kill Morgan, or has he already? It's been too long since her abduction." Her voice quivered. "I was so scared the remains we'd find were hers, but they weren't."

"You know that for sure?" Not that he didn't trust her qualified opinion, but his curiosity piqued.

"Well, there are a number of factors to consider, but the cooler weather would slow the decomposition process significantly." Her professional voice replaced her obvious earlier trepidation.

He turned his head toward her. "Don't think—"

"Look out!" Jordyn jolted forward and braced her hands against the dash.

Bones barked.

Colt shifted his eyes back to the road.

Headlights came precariously close to his SUV. He swerved right, barely missing the vehicle. "That was close. Too—"

Bones growled, then barked again, alerting them to more danger.

Colt's muscles tensed. High beams shone in the rearview mirror, blinding his vision moments before another vehicle rammed into the back of his SUV.

Jordyn screamed.

Colt white-knuckled the steering wheel and struggled to keep his cruiser on the winding road.

Crunch!

The driver rammed them again, pushing Colt's SUV toward the edge of the road.

Lord, save us!

The tires hit gravel, and Colt lost control, sending them over the embankment.

The SUV rolled, and Colt's head slammed into the deployed airbag.

Propelling him into darkness.

THIRTEEN

Barking echoed somewhere in the distance as Jordyn tried to open her eyes and shake the fog from her brain. Where was she? What happened? Nausea took over her gut, and the putrid taste of bile rested on her tongue. There was more barking, then the dog whined. Bones? Jordyn could smell gas fumes wafting near her, moments before a whoosh sounded. She jerked forward in her seat. The crash! She shook her head to clear her mind and blinked open her eyes. Smoke seeped into the SUV.

They had to escape. Now.

Colt's head lay lodged in the airbag, unmoving.

She clicked his seat belt button and released him, easing him backward. "Colt! Wake up." She shook him. "Come back to me."

She checked the front of the car. Smoke rose from the demolished hood, and flames shot upward, blocking her from getting to Colt's door that way. She'd have to go around the back.

Colt was unconscious.

It was up to Jordyn to save them.

She fumbled with her seat belt, and finally the mechanism unsnapped, a resounding click giving her freedom. She pushed the door open and fell onto the cool ground.

Her leg throbbed from the impact, but she ignored the pain and stumbled around to the vehicle's back, opening the tailgate and unlatching the dog crate. "Bones, come!"

Bones leaped from the vehicle and raced to Colt's side. He barked and clawed at the door, his intention clear.

Save his partner.

Jordyn tugged on Colt's door handle, but something had jammed the lock.

The flames grew higher, crawling toward the gas tank. They only had moments.

Lord, no! Save him. Please hear me!

She thrust her hip into the door as hard as her injured body allowed and tried again. This time it worked, and the door creaked open. She reached under Colt's arms and lugged him out. Ignoring the heat, she dragged him away from the burning SUV.

The flames billowed, chasing them deeper into the forest.

Bones barked as if telling her to move faster.

I'm trying, bud. I'm trying. Lord, give me strength.

Adrenaline fueled her muscles, and she scrambled farther from the flames.

She pulled him a safe distance and stopped beside a boulder just as the vehicle exploded, sending parts into the air along with a fireball. *Too close.* Was God looking out for them?

Jordyn slumped to the ground and held Colt in her arms, rocking him. "Come on, wake up. Please." Tears pooled as her feelings for him gushed out. *Don't leave me. Again.*

Bones barked and licked Colt's face.

Jordyn kissed Colt's forehead. "I miss you, my love." The term of endearment she'd used for him back when they were together. She held him tighter and hummed their favorite song, as if that would resonate somewhere inside him and call him back to consciousness.

Colt stirred, bringing hope to Jordyn. He was going to be okay. He had to be.

Bones licked him again.

Colt reached his hand up to his face and wiped. "Okay. I'm here, buddy." He blinked his eyes open. "What happened?"

Jordyn caressed his cheek. "Driver pushed us off the road. We rolled and hit a tree. I woke up, and the SUV was on fire. Got you and Bones out." She ran her hand down his arms. "Are you hurt anywhere?"

"I don't think so." He grazed her forehead. "You're bleeding."

"I'm fine. You okay to walk? We have to get to the road."

Bones growled and barreled forward.

Jordyn stiffened. "Something has him riled up. Come on. I'll help you stand." She pushed herself up and gripped Colt under his arms, hoisting him to his feet.

Bones barked.

Seconds later, a shot rang out as a bullet zinged over their heads.

"We gotta move!" Jordyn yelled.

Confusion distorted Colt's face.

She needed him to snap back to their situation. She shook him. "Come on, Colt."

Another bullet pinged off the boulder beside them.

Colt straightened and unleashed his Sig. "Bones, come!"

The dog scurried back to them.

Colt turned and pointed. "This way. Not sure exactly where we are, but we have to go deeper into the wilderness to outrun him."

"Can you walk?" She latched on to his arm.

"When someone is shooting at us? Yes." He unhooked the flashlight on his duty belt and handed it to her. "You light the way."

Together, they stumbled through the rocky terrain, sidestepping protruding tree stumps and roots. The group prodded through the bush, striving to outrun the perp behind them.

Jordyn suspected the BoneDigger had followed them and rammed them off the road. Who else would it have been? Obviously, once he'd realized he hadn't succeeded in killing them in other ways, he'd turned to bullets.

After ten minutes, they slowed their pace when no further shots sounded.

Somewhere ahead, Jordyn noted the sound of waves slapping the shoreline. She had to determine their location. She stopped running and shined the light ahead, examining the area. The beam revealed a rocky cliff near where they were walking. Not good. They were dangerously close to the ocean. If they had crashed here, they would have plummeted into the freezing water. Coincidence? Probably not. Her mother would call it a God thing.

You were looking out for us, weren't You, Lord?

Raindrops splattered on Jordyn's head. When would the weather turn in their favor? The rain would make the terrain slick, and she didn't want to risk slipping on the rocks. Great—rough going ahead, and a killer behind them. Terrible options. Where could they go?

Colt nudged her forward. "Keep walking. He might be still following us."

"I know, but there's a cliff right here, and the rain is making the rocks slippery." She reached into her pocket for her cell phone, but it wasn't there. *Ugh!* She'd dropped it on the floorboard before they were rammed. "My phone is in the cruiser. Do you have yours?"

He holstered his gun and unfastened his phone from the case attached to his belt, checking the screen. "No bars. Poor reception in this neck of the woods." He tried his radio. "That's not working either. Must have broken in the crash."

She peeked over her shoulder and caught a glimpse of billowing smoke from their accident. "Do you think someone will see the smoke and call 911?"

"Hopefully, but the suspect could be waiting in the wings. We've got to keep moving."

"But which way?" She turned the light in the opposite direction from the water. "Let's head away from the cliff."

Thirty minutes later, Jordyn stumbled but caught her footing. Her weary legs wouldn't take much more. She had to rest, but where?

They stepped into a small clearing.

A towering building stood on the edge of a cliff in the distance.

A lighthouse.

Could this be their safe haven until they could get help?

Colt's shoulders sagged, and his legs felt cemented into place as he and Jordyn studied the lighthouse at the cliff's edge. The abandoned tower still stood tall, but would it keep them safe?

And did they have a choice? He tried his cell phone again. Still no signal. He fought the urge to throw the device, counting to ten instead. They were now far from the highway, with no cell bars. The rain had turned into a downpour, and they were soaked. Tired. Frustrated. He looked again at the lighthouse. He racked his brain trying to remember the history behind the keeper who had once lived there.

"Do you think we could take refuge in there?" Jordyn asked.

"I'm not sure, and I was just wondering that too. Do you remember how long since it's been operational?"

"Didn't they build a new one farther down the highway? I remember coming to this place as a kid, and it had been boarded up then." She shined the light at the dilapidated tower.

Planks had been nailed across the front door, and a corner in the upper window was broken. The larger lighthouse had once provided living quarters for keepers back in the day.

Woof! Bones rubbed against Colt's leg.

Colt leaned down and patted his dog. "I know, buddy. You're tired too." He willed his weary legs forward. "Let's check it out."

They approached the lighthouse.

Jordyn shined the beam over the exterior, trailing it higher. "If we can get inside and to the top, perhaps you can get a cell signal."

"Maybe. But first, we need to remove the boards and break in."

Jordyn chuckled. "*Breaking and entering.* Terminology I bet you never thought you'd use when referring to yourself, huh?"

"Sometimes you gotta do what you gotta do." He inched closer to the door and ran his fingers along the planks. "Okay, they've rotted throughout the years, so maybe with both of us pulling, we can get in."

Jordyn set the flashlight faceup on the cement walkway, the beam shining upward. She positioned herself beside him. "Okay, ready."

They both placed their fingers under the board.

Colt counted. "One, two, three. Now!"

They tugged, and the board came loose. The momentum thrust them backward, and they fell with a thud.

"Oof!" Jordyn laughed.

Bones barked.

Colt rubbed his backside. "Okay, let's not do that again." He pushed himself upright and threw the board around the corner, out of sight from anyone who had perhaps followed them. He then tried the rickety handle. Locked. He wiggled the knob and thrust his shoulder into the decaying door at the same time.

It broke, and Colt stumbled into the lighthouse. Dust and cobwebs greeted him. He turned from the entrance. "You sure you want to come in? I know you hate creepy-crawly things." She had shared her fear of bugs, especially spiders, when they'd talked about camping.

She hesitated as the rain intensified.

Bones trotted inside and turned, barking. His cue for her to follow.

"I hear ya, bud," she said. "I don't have a choice, do I?"

The dog shook off his wet fur and trotted farther inside the circular building.

"Okay, I'm coming." Jordyn grabbed the flashlight and trudged through the half-broken door. "If memory serves me correctly, there's a room on the upper level before the light at the top."

"How often did you come here?" Colt asked.

"Morgan and I..." She hesitated and shined the light upward. "We used to race each other to the top. That was back when the authorities left it open. Until kids vandalized it, of course."

Colt shoved the door closed, fastening the broken hinges as much as he could, concealing their entrance into the tower. "Shine the light at the stairs. I want to be sure they're safe before we climb."

She directed the beam onto the staircase.

He placed his foot on the first step. It held, so he pushed more weight onto it. It creaked but didn't give way. "Okay, let me go first. Hand me the light."

She obeyed.

"Stay close." Colt pointed the light up the steps. "Bones, come."

The dog bounded up the stairs like a kid, as if excited to get to the top to find some sort of prize.

Colt shook his head at his dog's antics, clutched the wobbly railing and proceeded cautiously. The adrenaline had subsided, and his sluggish legs labored with each step. The crash had taken more out of him than he'd thought. *God, please let this tower of refuge keep us safe.*

They both required rest if they were to outrun any more of the BoneDigger's bullets.

Jordyn thrashed, hovering between the dream world and consciousness. The hazy images pulled her under, and she found herself in a car. Her father took the turn too fast, and Jordyn's tiny five-year-old hands grabbed the car seat's edge. "Papa! Slower. I'm scared." Snowflakes danced on the windshield as she peered between the seats. The darkness hid the lines on the road ahead, but the icy conditions glistened in the headlights. The car swerved, and a raggedy, bearded man appeared in the headlights. She pointed and screamed. "Papa. Man!"

Her father said a bad word and stomped on the brake.

She lurched forward as the car tried to stop, but the thud told her little brain they'd just hit him.

They started to skid, and she caught a glimpse

of the man lying in the road before the car careened into a motion she wanted to forget.

Spinning, spinning, spinning.

"Papa, stop!"

The sound of her own scream woke her. Jordyn jerked up from the lumpy cot, her heart jackhammering as she tried to make sense of the nightmare. Realization dawned on her.

It wasn't a dream. It had happened years ago, and that frightful night was now clear as day.

Her father had hit a man and never stopped.

Bones barked before nudging his nose in her face, offering comfort.

Colt appeared at her side. "Jordyn, you okay?"

She shook her head, the words lodged in her throat.

He sat on the cot and brought her into an embrace.

She sobbed and sobbed, unable to suppress the experience and all her fears any longer.

Bones nestled on the other side as Colt rocked her in comfort. "Shh... You're okay. It's just a dream. It's gonna be fine."

Would it? She now remembered what she'd buried for years. Her father's hit-and-run accident.

The mistake he'd wanted her to forget...forever.

She stopped crying and pushed back, then slowly rose to her feet. "You don't understand. Yes, it was a dream, but it was something that happened to me when I was five. I remember now." She willed her legs forward and straggled over to the small room's window.

Light shone through the distant trees. Daybreak was on the cusp of presenting itself—but would it bring the sun or more clouds? She needed a ray of hope after the darkness.

She'd obviously slept for a few hours after they had sought refuge in the lighthouse. The room housed a single cot, a chair and a table. Not much space, but enough for them to retreat from the BoneDigger.

Colt had insisted she lie down on the cot and get some rest, while he sat in the chair. He had tried calling for help but still couldn't get a signal. They'd planned to wait out the rain and leave on foot in the morning. They'd hike out to the highway and try calling for help from there.

Colt placed his hand on her back. "Tell me about it."

She'd failed to hear his approach and turned, startled. His nearness forced out the breath she'd been holding, and she struggled to concentrate. Even his smoky scent from the crash didn't deter her from the moment. She wanted to reach out and caress his handsome face, linger at his chin dimple. However, it wasn't the time or the place.

Would it ever be?

She stowed away that thought and braced her hands at her side. "My father and I were out shopping for Christmas presents for Mom and Morgan. I wanted to buy something special for them with my allowance, so I had asked him to take me to the store. On the way home, we got caught in a snowstorm. I remember Dad was driving too fast, and suddenly, an older man stood in the middle of the road. Dad hit the brakes, and we spun." She stopped, gathering the cloudy, emerging thoughts from that night. "Then I heard a terrible sound."

"What?"

"A thud. Dad had hit the man but failed to stop and check on him. The last thing I remember is seeing a body lying on the road."

"Why didn't your father stop?"

"I don't know. That was when he was just going into politics." She gulped. "Wait… I remember him pointing his finger at me and telling me never to say anything. Said it was our little secret."

"What? He asked a five-year-old to keep a crime a secret?"

The image of her father's face from that night flashed in her mind. "I finally remember everything clearly, and I won't forget the look on his face. It was almost…" She couldn't say the word.

Colt placed his hands on her upper arms. "Almost what?"

"Evil," she whispered.

The darkness of that night lingered in her mind. Recently, her father had been talking about his past mistakes. Had that triggered her memory? No wonder she had recently retreated into a murky place. "I have to get home and confront him. To see if the man lived. I don't like that Dad kept this from me and made me keep it too. I hate secrets."

"I'm sorry you went through that, Jordyn." Colt traced his finger along her jawline.

Something he always did when they'd been together.

She shivered from his gesture and stared into his eyes. *I want you back in my life.* Though she longed to say those words out loud, she kept them to herself. Betrayal from Tyler's indiscretion and Colt's abandonment held her back.

Their eyes locked, and Jordyn wished at that moment she possessed the superpower to read minds. *What are you thinking?*

His gaze dropped to her lips.

Was he going to kiss her?

Did she *want* him to kiss her?

More than anything.

He averted his gaze out the window and stepped away, breaking the moment.

It was obvious.

He no longer loved her.

And never would.

FOURTEEN

Colt dug his nails into his palms to curb the desire to kiss Jordyn. He had almost given in but remembered her wish for children. Colt saw the disappointment pass over her face. He had a faint memory of her saying she missed him back when they were at the accident site. Or had he dreamed that? Plus, her comment about hating secrets tugged at his heart. Should he tell her the real reason he'd broken up with her? How he struggled with insecurities and failure?

He took her hands in his. "Jordyn, I'm sorry. I need to tell—"

She snatched her hands out of his, pursing her lips. "It's okay. No need to explain. Your actions are obvious. Let's move out and get back to the highway." She pivoted, grabbed her coat and headed toward the stairs.

Ugh! Colt couldn't do anything right these days. "Bones, guard. Jordyn, wait for me."

His K-9 accompanied his charge, his claws clicking on the wood floor.

Colt followed down the stairs and unholstered his weapon before edging the door open. The dawn light had begun its ascent, but Colt still couldn't get a clear picture of the perimeter. He turned to Jordyn. "Stay here with Bones. I'm going to walk around the area to ensure we're alone. Okay?"

Minutes later, he gave her an all-clear sign, and they set out. After an hour's hike, they reached the highway.

Colt withdrew his cell phone and checked the bars. "Finally. A signal." He tapped the speed dial number for his leader and waited.

"Peters! Where have you been? I've been trying to reach you." Sergeant Warren's breathless voice indicated he'd either been anxious or running. "We found your charred cruiser after someone called in the accident. I'm here with the other constables. Where are you?"

"We're approximately six kilometers east of the accident site."

"Are you all okay? What happened?"

"Yes. We were rammed off the road and then rolled. Jordyn managed to get us all out before the SUV blew."

"So why are you so far away?"

Colt leaned against a tree near the road. "Because the suspect shot at us after they saw we were alive. We took refuge in the old lighthouse. We made it out to the highway this morning, and we need a pickup. Can you bring water? We're all parched, including Bones."

"Okay. Stay put. On my way." The sergeant ended the call.

Colt eyed Jordyn. She huddled with Bones on a large rock alongside the road. She stared off into the distance, a haggard expression consuming her pretty face.

You did this, Colt.

He exhaled and approached. "Sergeant Warren will be here soon. He's at the accident site."

"Good. I need to get a new cell phone on the way back to Dad's. I have to check in with my team. They're probably waiting for me at the new grave."

He handed her his phone. "Use mine for now."

"Thanks." She took the device and left to make the call.

Ten minutes later, Sergeant Warren's cruiser parked along the side of the road. He exited his vehicle and rushed forward. "So glad you're okay. I was worried when we didn't find you near the accident." He looked from Colt to Jordyn. "Okay, you both look exhausted. I'm ordering you to take some time to recoup. Do you want me to take you to the premier's cottage?" He handed them each a bottle of water.

"Yes." Colt rubbed the stubble on his chin. "But I've had enough rest. We need to find Morgan's sister."

"Other constables are working on that."

Jordyn stepped forward. "It's been too long. Have you had any viable leads?" She passed Colt his phone.

"I'm sorry to say, none have panned out. Most have been from people just wanting the reward money."

Jordyn clung to the sergeant's arm. "Find her. Please. I need my sister back. Someone must have seen something."

"We're working on it, giving it our number one priority. I promise." He turned back to Colt. "We received the guard's blood test results. He was drugged with a mild sedative. Seems like someone wanted to knock him out but not kill him."

Colt took a swig of water before tipping it in front of Bones's mouth. The K-9 lapped it up. "Perhaps he's not the victim type the BoneDigger is looking for."

The sergeant crossed his arms. "Do we even know his MO?"

"Not until we hear all results from Dr. Chambers," Colt said. "Jordyn, any idea of when that will be?"

"He told me he's working around the clock with the other MEs and Dr. Jones, our chief ME. A bit unorthodox, but it should speed up the process. Maybe in a few days?" She paused. "But this isn't television. Things don't happen in an hour."

Her tone was edgy, and Colt guessed that she

was frustrated at him over their earlier intimate moment. He shouldn't have gotten so close, but the urge to kiss her had consumed him.

"Although, Vance told me my father's office is pressuring him to finish sooner rather than later."

Colt bristled. Why did her use of the ME's first name prickle his nerves? *Focus.*

The sergeant clapped. "Okay, time to go. You both can't function without proper rest." He pointed to Colt. "And you can continue to work out of the premier's residence. Stay away from the station, or I will bust you."

Colt chuckled. The fiftysomething sergeant had always treated him like a son, and now wasn't any different. "Fine, but can we stop at my place on the way there? I need some things and more of Bones's special dog food."

Bones barked.

Sergeant Warren chuckled. "Seems he agrees. Jordyn, anything you need?"

"Yes, a new cell phone," Jordyn said. "Mine was in the SUV when it blew."

"Sure thing. Let's go before—"

A news van pulled in behind the sergeant's cruiser.

Great. Ursula Baine again.

She hopped out from the van and sprinted toward them, her cameraman following.

"Let me handle this." Sergeant Warren raised his hands. "That's far enough, Miss Baine. How many times do we need to remind you that we can't comment on an ongoing investigation?"

She raised her microphone toward Colt. "Constable Peters, why haven't you told the public your brother, Lincoln Peters, was among the BoneDigger's victims?"

What? Where had she obtained that information? Colt peeked at Jordyn.

Her open mouth told him that she, too, was shocked at Ursula's question.

He turned back to the reporter. "Where are you getting your information?"

"You know I can't reveal my sources. So…is it true?"

Bones growled.

His dog also didn't like the reporter. *You're an excellent judge of character, partner.*

Sergeant Warren placed his hand over the woman's microphone. "No comment. Please leave." He addressed Colt and Jordyn. "Get in the cruiser."

In the midafternoon, after getting himself checked out at the hospital and Bones at the vet, Colt carried two coffees into the dining room, where Jordyn worked. He had also picked up his police-issued laptop, and Sergeant Warren had arranged for another SUV to be delivered to their location. Colt had rewarded Bones with a scrumptious doggy meal and the K-9 had devoured the food.

They each had snagged a few extra hours' rest at his sergeant's strong recommendation. After cleaning up, Colt had changed into jeans and a blue-and-green-plaid shirt. The comfy clothes, rather than his uniform, helped him relax.

A little.

They still had to find Morgan, figure out the BoneDigger's MO and catch him.

No pressure.

He set a pumpkin spice latte by Jordyn. "Your fave."

Would the beverage put him back in her good graces or at least open the door to the possibility?

He brought a treat out of his pocket and gave it to Bones. The dog had taken up residence under Jordyn's chair—his way of protecting her.

Jordyn removed her reading glasses and cupped the latte in her hands, sipping. "So good. Thanks."

He took a drink of his dark roast and peeked over her shoulder. "What are you working on?"

"Reviewing our documentation on the victims."

Colt sat in the chair opposite her and opened his laptop. "I'm going to look at our police reports." He hesitated. "I don't understand how Ursula keeps getting information we haven't released to the public. Who's her source?"

"Do you think it could be someone on our teams?"

"I certainly hope not." He logged into his secure network. "That would mean—"

His cell phone buzzed, interrupting him. Unknown caller. His finger hovered over Accept, contemplating whether he should take the call.

"You gonna get that?" Jordyn asked.

He hit the button and put the call on speaker. "Constable Peters here."

"'Bout time you picked up," a distorted voice said.

Colt straightened in his chair and glanced at Jordyn.

Her widened eyes told Colt the caller had captured her undivided attention as well.

"Who's this?" Colt asked.

"Who do you think? Is the lovely Dr. Miller with you?"

Jordyn flew out of her seat. "Where is my sister?" she asked, yelling into the phone.

"Patience, patience. We'll get to that. First, I need to tell you a story."

Bones bounded out from under Jordyn's seat and barked at the phone, baring his teeth.

Colt opened his recorder app on his laptop, hitting the record button. He wanted to study the caller's voice carefully. See if there were words or phrases he used that might identify him.

"Aw… Bones is there too. Good. Now that I

have your attention, let me tell you I didn't kidnap the wrong Miller twin. I knew exactly who my associate took."

Jordyn balled up her hands into fists. "Why? Why do you want Morgan? What did she do to you?"

"Nothing."

"Then take me. I'll give myself up if you let her go."

Colt grimaced and hit the mute button. "What are you doing? You can't do that."

"She has two little girls. I don't." She moved closer to Colt and unmuted his phone. "Tell me where I can meet you."

"You don't get it. I don't want either of you. Your father needs to pay for his sin."

Terror was etched on Jordyn's face. "What are you talking about?"

"I know who your father hit that night long ago."

Jordyn gasped. "What? How is that connected to you?"

"That's my secret. You tell your father to confess his sin publicly within the next forty-eight hours, or Morgan dies."

Jordyn slammed her hand on the table. "It's not her fault!"

Bones barked.

"Just do as I say, and she won't get hurt."

Colt placed his hand on top of Jordyn's, hoping

to calm her temper. "Who are all the remains you buried, and why did you kill them?"

Jordyn drew her hand away and slouched in her chair, arms folded.

"Another mystery for you to solve, Constable Peters. I will tell you this—I learned my trade from the best. Each death was for a specific reason."

Colt clenched his hands into fists too. "What reason could you possibly have had to kill my brother?"

"Let's just say he was in the wrong place at the wrong time." He clucked his tongue. "Oh. The new grave you found? You don't need to examine it. I can tell you it's my dear old grandfather, and he died of natural causes. Pity. He deserved a harsher death."

Jordyn's gaze shot to Colt's.

A ticking clock filtered through the phone. "Your father's time starts now. Remember, forty-eight hours."

The call dropped.

Colt stopped his recording. "Well, an interesting turn of events. We need to get your father here now." He pushed himself to his feet. "I'm calling Sergeant Warren to update him."

Jordyn buried her head in her hands. "Morgan is as good as dead."

"Why do you say that?"

She looked up, her terror-stricken eyes flashing. "Because Premier Russell Miller doesn't negotiate with terrorists. Not even if his family's lives are on the line."

Colt dropped back into his chair with one thought emerging.

It was up to him to find Morgan and catch the BoneDigger before he killed an innocent woman.

Jordyn paced in her father's living room, waiting for him to return to his residence. She had placed a panicked call to his office when neither of her parents answered their phones, and his assistant said she would get the message to the premier as soon as his important meeting ended. The woman had refused to interrupt her father, even after Jordyn told her it was a matter of life and death. She clenched her hands into fists and positioned herself in front of the window to watch for his return. She checked her watch. It had been nearly two hours since the BoneDigger had called. They were wasting precious time. *Dad, why haven't you come home yet? Don't your daughters mean more to you than work?*

Colt had sequestered himself in the dining room, conferring with his sergeant and going over his fellow police officers' reports for any information that may help the situation. He had sent the audio file of the BoneDigger's call to Forensics, hoping for a lead.

A black SUV appeared around the bend of her

father's cottage, followed by another car—her father's security detail.

Where was your security detail when the Bone-Digger abducted Morgan, Dad?

Jordyn chewed on her lip. Her anger had gotten the best of her, and she needed to curb her feelings. She was aware of her father's responsibilities to the province, as well as both Morgan's and Jordyn's requests for privacy. They had been followed all their lives and wanted freedom.

But would that freedom now cost them everything?

The front door slammed, and a scurry of footfalls pounded on the hardwood floor.

Bones jumped up from his nearby position and growled.

"It's okay, bud. Just Dad."

Bones wagged his tail at her.

At least the dog paid attention to Jordyn.

Colt emerged through the French doors connecting the living room and dining room. "Your father back?"

"Just arrived. Finally."

"Where's your mom?"

"With him." Jordyn moved over by the fireplace. She needed warmth to take the chill away—not from the cool fall day but from her iced nerves. "I'm not sure how much of this accident she knows about."

"Understood. I'll let you do the talking."

"Jordyn, where are you?" her father yelled from the hallway.

She steeled her jaw, bracing herself for confrontation. "In the living room."

Her parents hurried into the room, followed by Ted and Oscar. Her father's two burly guards stood ready to block anyone from getting to the premier.

It will take more than them to stop me from learning the truth, Dad.

Her mother opened her arms and wrapped them around Jordyn. "We heard you were in a frantic state. What's going on?"

Jordyn held her mother out at arm's length. "Let's all sit." She turned to her father, pointing to his men. "Dad, just family."

Her father gestured toward Colt. "What about him?"

"I can go, Jordyn." He got up to leave, but Jordyn latched on to his hand.

"He stays." She went over to the couch, dragging Colt with her. She may not have the man's love, but she needed his strong presence right now.

"Sir, I'm not comfortable leaving you," Ted said.

Her father raised his hand. "It's okay, Ted. I'll be fine. Go, please. It seems my daughter requires my undivided attention."

Jordyn's mother sat in the rocker. "Tell us what has you upset."

"Sit, Dad." Jordyn pointed to the chair across from the couch.

"I prefer to stand."

"Fine." Jordyn gathered her words carefully. "Tell me what happened that winter night when I was five and you hit a man with your car."

Her mother leaned forward, eyes widening.

Her father's jaw dropped.

A hush permeated the room, with only the crackling fire to serve as a backdrop to the awkward silence.

Jordyn gave him a minute to let her question sink in before continuing. She hated to be so dramatic, but she needed answers—and fast. "Yes, I remember now. But I want to hear what happened from your lips, Dad." She hesitated. "Because your other daughter's life depends on it."

Her mother leaped to her feet. "What is she talking about, Russell? What accident?" She addressed Colt, "Did you find Morgan?"

Colt hung his head. "I'm afraid not."

"You never knew, Mom?" Jordyn asked.

A long sigh slipped from her father's mouth before he sank into a chair. "I told her I hit a deer that night." He addressed his wife, "Love, please sit."

Fran Miller listened to her husband and sat back in the rocking chair. A strained expression weathered her pretty face as she waited for his story.

Jordyn's father fiddled with the buttons on his overcoat as if gathering his thoughts. "It was close to Christmas. Jordyn had requested I take her to the store. She wanted to buy you and Morgan a special present with her allowance." He wiggled out of his coat and tossed it on a chair. "After an hour of going up and down all the rows, Jordyn finally selected her gifts. While we were in the store, an unexpected snowstorm hit, so the roads were slick. It was when we lived on the east side of town," he explained. After swallowing hard, he continued, "A man came out of nowhere, and I tried to brake, but we skidded and… I hit him."

"What?" her mother asked. "Was he okay?"

Jordyn rose and fingered her nieces' picture on the mantel. "You didn't just hit him—you left him there and didn't stop." She pivoted to face her father. "Right, Dad?"

He slumped in his chair. "Yes."

Jordyn couldn't restrain her anger. "And then you made me swear not to tell anyone."

Her mother hopped to her feet once more. "Why, Russell? Why would you do that?"

"Because it was the year I entered politics, and I couldn't risk the scandal. You know how it would have looked."

Jordyn approached her mother and urged her to sit. "I'm sorry you had to find out this way, Mom." She turned to her father. "Do you know what happened to the man?"

He nodded. "I followed the news and the police report. The man didn't die but was paralyzed. I sent a cashier's check to cover any medical expenses and a note apologizing." He pushed himself out of his chair and paced the room. "I'm ashamed of it all, but after time went on, I buried everything."

"How could you, Russell? What would God say to your actions?" Her mother's voice boomed in the living room.

Bones lifted his head.

Her father pinched the bridge of his nose and closed his eyes. "Don't you think I know that? I've regretted it all my life."

"Well, Dad, somehow, the BoneDigger knows all about your little secret, and if you don't air it publicly to your constituents within the next forty-eight hours, Morgan will die." She checked her watch. "Forty-six hours now."

Her parents both flew to their feet.

"What has she got to do with this?" her father asked.

"No idea, but he called Colt's phone and gave us his demands."

Her father's gaze traveled over to Colt. "Are you able to find my daughter?"

"We've tried, sir. You need to do as he says."

Tears filled the normally stoic man's eyes as he plopped back into his chair. "I can't."

"Why, Dad?" Jordyn asked.

"Because the news would put me out of office and stop some very important work I'm doing."

Her mother's knees buckled, and she dropped to the floor.

Jordyn's face flushed as her anger rose. "Your job is more important than your own daughter?"

"You don't understand, Pooh Bear." He rushed to his wife's side and brought her into his arms, rocking her as she sobbed. "This work will save thousands of lives. I can't put one life above thousands, even if it is my daughter's." His voice quivered at his last statement.

Jordyn fell onto the couch, burying her head in Colt's chest. Through her sorrow, questions rose in her mind.

What did Morgan's life have to do with the BoneDigger? What was the connection?

FIFTEEN

Colt held Jordyn tight, resting his chin on the top of her head as scenarios of how to save this family from agony tumbled through his mind. However, nothing emerged. He didn't understand how the BoneDigger knew about the man Russell had struck all those years ago. Colt replayed their conversation in his head, pondering the premier's account of what had happened that night. *Wait...*

Colt's muscles locked. "You said you lived on the east side of Charock Harbour back then?"

Jordyn lifted her head from his chest. "Yes, why?"

"Mr. Miller, what road did this happen on?" Colt asked.

"Old Harbour Road," Russell replied. "It's no longer used as much, since we built the new highway."

Colt shot off the couch, jarring Jordyn from his arms.

Bones barked, once again sensing Colt's changed demeanor.

"What are you thinking, Colt?" Jordyn asked, pushing herself to her feet.

"Old Harbour Road is where I left Linc that night ten years ago, and it's not that far from the cemetery. Is it possible that the BoneDigger lives around there and saw what happened that night?"

She scratched her forehead. "I don't know."

"What if he was a child—like you—and witnessed it?"

"Possibly." Jordyn grabbed his arm. "You have to get constables to re-canvass that area. Perhaps Morgan is being held on a farm along that road."

"It may be a long shot or the break we need." Colt dug out his phone. "Calling my sergeant now." He punched in the man's speed dial number as he ran into the dining room.

"Peters, what's going on?" his sergeant asked.

"Listen, we need to canvass the farms around Old Harbour Road. I have reason to believe that the BoneDigger may live in that area. Plus, it was also the road where my brother went missing years ago."

"I'm pretty sure officers did that when your family reported Lincoln's disappearance."

Colt fingered Jordyn's documents on the dining room table, scanning her findings on the victims. He stopped at Linc's name—the only remains they had identified. "I feel there's some kind of link between all the victims and Morgan's kidnapping. Can we send constables to re-canvass?"

"Where's this coming from, son?"

Colt tightened his lips. How much could he say? He didn't like keeping secrets from his boss, but it wasn't his story to tell. "Do you trust me?"

"Implicitly."

"I can't say where the lead came from, but I think it's valid and we have to follow up. All will be revealed soon. In the meantime, I'm going to get the premier to call the ME again. We need those other identities." He paused. "Something in my gut is telling me they're the key."

"Understood. We're stretched thin right now." A wheeze sailed through the phone. "However, I'll send Constable Greer to that area and report back."

"I can help too," Colt said.

"You can't. Your job is protection for the premier's daughter."

He gripped his cell phone tighter. "But Morgan *is* the premier's daughter."

"You know what I mean. You and Bones are assigned to Jordyn."

Colt knew his boss was right. Another question rose. "Did Forensics get anything off the recording I sent?"

"Sorry, dead end."

Figures. "Not surprised. Okay, tell Greer to

be on alert at all times. Someone on one of those farms is connected. Somehow."

"Will do. Stay safe."

Colt pocketed his phone and returned to the Millers. "Russell, can you call the ME's office and give him a little nudge, personally?"

Jordyn's eyes narrowed. "Vance already knows the importance of finishing his examinations."

"I realize that, but I feel at least one of those remains holds the key we need."

Russell released his wife and rose. "I'm on it." He shuffled out of the room.

"Sergeant Warren is sending Constable Greer to canvass the farms along Old Harbour Road. Maybe they missed something years ago, when they were investigating Linc's disappearance."

"Just one constable?" Jordyn asked. "There are many farms out there. Some are abandoned, but they're a tight community and somewhat odd."

"Unfortunately, everyone else is tied up with other investigations. We're a small station." Her last comment finally registered in his brain. "Wait, you said they're odd. How? I don't remember that as a kid."

"There were a few farms that held private church gatherings."

"You mean like a cult?"

"No, just a group who wanted to worship together and not in a big congregation." She helped her mother onto the couch. "They hold home church services."

Her comment sparked a memory that ignited a thought. "Remember how the BoneDigger positioned the graves? Did Nick ever look into rituals?"

Her eyes brightened. "You're right. I'll check with him. But first, I'm gonna take Mom to her bedroom. She needs to rest."

"Understood. Meanwhile, I'm going to call our persistent reporter and have a little chat."

"To find out her source?"

"Yup. And offer her an exclusive if she helps."

"Good. I'll be back in a few minutes." Jordyn guided her mother from the room with Bones by her side.

Good boy. I trained you well.

Colt hurried into the dining room, where he'd left all his information, and rummaged through until he found Ursula's number. He keyed it into his phone and waited.

Her chipper voice practically sang through the line. "Ursula Baine of Charock Channel 5 News speaking. How can I help you?"

"Miss Baine, this is Constable Peters. May I have a moment of your time?" he asked.

"Certainly. You have information for me?"

Colt pulled out a chair and sat. "I have a question for you, and I need you to be honest. Lives depend on your answer."

"This sounds interesting. What's your question?"

"Who told you about the lynx carvings and my brother?"

"I can't reveal—"

"What if I offer you an exclusive interview?" he cut in, resisting the urge to roll his eyes at her usual excuse.

Silence.

He'd caught her attention.

"Okay," she finally said. "On one condition."

That didn't sound good. "Shoot."

"That our fearless premier tells us what dreadful secret he's hiding."

Colt froze. How did she know that, too? This woman was insufferable. "That's not something I can help you with." He would not betray the Miller family. "Let me guess—the same informant told you this information?"

"Perhaps."

"Did your source also tell you what the secret was?"

"No, only that all would be revealed soon."

Wait... Colt popped to his feet, thinking about the timing of their past conversations. "Your source *is* the BoneDigger, isn't it?" It was the only thing that made sense.

Silence once again filtered through the phone.

Her way of saying yes.

"I'll take your silence as confirmation. Thank you."

"So, do I get an exclusive?" she asked.

"I'll be in touch." He punched off, not committing to anything.

Determined thumping footsteps approached. Colt turned around.

Jordyn almost skidded into the room, raising her cell phone. "That was Vance. He's not happy my dad pressured him, but I explained a little as to why. His team is almost done."

"Good news." He tossed his phone on the table. "Ursula pretty much confirmed her source is the BoneDigger."

Jordyn's jaw dropped. "What?"

"I guessed it after she mentioned she wanted to know what your father was hiding. She didn't deny it."

Jordyn fell into a nearby chair, shock settling on her ashen face. "She knows Dad hit a man?"

"I don't think so. Just that he has a secret."

Jordyn gnawed on her lip. "Well, we can use her if Dad does a press conference. Morgan's life depends on it."

The next forty-some hours would be interesting.

Ticktock. Ticktock.

The dining room grandfather clock towering in the corner chimed two o'clock, as if mocking them.

Colt prayed the constable sent to Old Harbour Road would help shed some light on their dangerous situation.

Before the BoneDigger made good on his promise.

Jordyn wiggled her foot under the table as she perused the links Nick had sent her regarding rituals, college hazings and more than she'd ever wanted to see. So much had changed since she'd gone to college, and that wasn't long ago. It had been thirty hours since the BoneDigger's demand was made, and the Honorable Premier Miller still hadn't relented. Time was wasting, and her sister's life lay on the line. Jordyn pounded the table, sending her coffee mug crashing to the floor.

Bones jumped up and barked.

"Sorry, bud. Didn't mean to startle you." She rushed into the kitchen, then came back with a broom and dish towel to clean up her mess.

Colt appeared in the doorway. "What's going on? I heard a crash."

"Only my temper flaring up."

"Still no success in convincing your father?" He took the broom from her hand and swept the broken pieces into a pile.

"Nope. He's so stubborn. I can't believe Sara found nothing at the farmhouses." Jordyn's lunch hardened in her stomach.

"Well, I'm not surprised. She told me it's a

close-knit community that looks after each other. She feels someone is hiding something, though. Their answers were curt and all the same, like they had all gathered to rehearse what they'd say."

"Not good. I looked at the links Nick sent me regarding rituals and hazing. Nothing really stands out. But I think you may be on to something. The carvings showed Bible verses. I assumed the placement of the graves in a circle was part of a religious ritual or something." Jordyn held the dustpan in place as Colt brushed the pieces into it. "Or maybe there's no significance at all and we're barking up the wrong proverbial tree."

Colt wiped the coffee from the floor with the dish towel, then took the dustpan into the kitchen. He returned moments later. "Another thought..." He moved to his laptop and turned it in her direction. "I just remembered something about the lynx carvings." He enlarged an image of one on his screens and pointed. "Look here."

She leaned closer. "I see it—a circle around the lynx's paw. Are the others the same?"

He pulled up the others one by one, enlarging them.

Jordyn whistled and slouched. "They do. What does it mean?"

"At first, I assumed the carver's hand slipped, but it has to mean something." He turned his laptop back around. "I'm going to search the internet and see what comes up. Just a sec."

She waited, tapping her thumb on the table. Patience had never been her strong suit.

"Okay, here's something. Some sites say the circle symbolizes forever since it has no beginning or end. Another says it's a completion."

"Circle of life. So the BoneDigger placed the graves in a circle to signify his completion of killing? Or completion of life?"

Colt slammed his laptop closed. "None of this makes sense."

Her computer dinged, announcing an email. "I think that's Vance's reports. He told me he'd have them today." She wiggled her mouse. "Yes! Okay, I need to read these. Then I'll let you know everything."

Colt stood. "I'm going to get us some coffee." He left the room.

Jordyn opened the documentation and slowly analyzed Vance and his team's findings, jotting down notes as she read. She didn't want to make any mistakes.

Colt returned, carrying two mugs. He set one to the right of her makeshift desk. "Fuel for you. Double cream, no sugar."

She smiled. "Thank you. You remembered."

"Of course." He took a seat opposite her and reopened his laptop.

For the next five minutes, she tried to ignore

his presence and concentrate on the task at hand. When she'd finished reading the report, she whistled.

Colt peeked at her over his screen. "What?"

"Okay, in a nutshell, here's what Vance determined. All five remains had fractures consistent with some sort of questionable trauma, indicating they were all killed. Three victims were shot. One was killed by blunt force to the head. The other was strangled or died of another form of neck trauma." She tapped her pen on the table. "It would take a strong person to do that. I noted the observation in my findings—but of course, I couldn't give the manner or cause of death."

"Which victim was that?"

"The older woman in her early seventies." She hesitated. "Wait, that woman's bones were more decomposed, with environmental markings, showing she'd possibly been dead for years." She ran her finger down her laptop's screen. "Plus, we know the newest grave is the BoneDigger's grandfather, and he died naturally. If we can believe him, that is."

"Any identities?"

"All but one. It looks like a family. Last name of Hickey. Then there's Lincoln. Vance is still waiting for a positive identification on the other male victim. Age range on him is thirty-five to forty."

Colt sprang out of his chair. "Wait, did you say Hickey?"

"Yes."

He typed something on his laptop, picked it up and placed the screen in front of her, pointing. "Look at this. There's a farmhouse along Old Harbour Road previously owned by a Jacob Hickey. I found it when I was looking into records. And it's adjacent to where my family lives. Just through the woods. We used to walk along the stone divider but didn't know the family. They kept to themselves and never allowed anyone near them, so we avoided the property for the most part."

"Perhaps Jacob Hickey is the grandfather the BoneDigger referred to." She paused. "You're thinking Lincoln cut through the property on his way home?"

Colt snapped his fingers. "Yes! Remember, the BoneDigger said Linc was in the wrong place at the wrong time. My guess is, he witnessed someone being killed and paid the price."

"You said the area had a close-knit community. A circle of like-minded people, so to speak." Jordyn bolted to her feet. "We have to get to that farmhouse. Now."

"I'm gonna request Greer meet us there." He pulled up short. "I know my boss told me my job was only to protect you, but I have to get to the bottom of this. Stopping the BoneDigger *is* protecting you."

"I'm coming too. Don't try to stop me. I have to find Morgan. Time is running out, and clearly Dad isn't going to confess."

Colt hesitated, then turned to his dog. "Bones, come."

Thirty minutes later, Jordyn followed Colt over to Sara's cruiser at the Hickey farm, with Bones at her heels.

"Thanks for coming, Greer." Colt shook her hand. "Did you get to talk to the property owner?"

"No one answered when I knocked earlier." She placed her hands on her hips. "You think this farm has some kind of significance to your brother's disappearance?"

"Yes, and to the BoneDigger's case." Colt went on to share with her what they'd found.

"But we can't go in there without a warrant. What do you expect to gain?" Sara asked.

"I just want to talk to the owner. If we feel they're hiding something, we'll try to obtain a warrant." Colt gripped his sidearm.

A thirty-ish woman with her hair wrapped in a bandana stomped onto her porch.

The group approached the home. Colt and Sara flashed their badges.

"Good afternoon. I'm Constable Peters. This is Constable Greer and Dr. Miller."

"What can I do for you?" The woman tilted her head, a smile curling her lips upward.

Was she flirting with an officer? Specifically, the handsome Colt Peters?

Brazen.

"We're wondering if you knew a Jacob Hickey," Sara said.

Her smile faded. "Never heard of him."

Why the change in expression?

Bones growled. Apparently, he agreed that something was off.

"Can I get your name?" Colt asked.

"Viv Winters."

"How long have you lived here, Miss Winters? Or is it *Mrs.* Winters?" Colt pulled a notebook from his pocket.

"It's *Miss*, and I bought this place six months ago." She stared at the ground.

Jordyn peeked at Colt.

His jaw twitched—an indicator of his agitation she remembered from when they had dated.

He also guessed the woman was lying.

"Can we come inside and talk?" Sara asked.

Viv crossed her arms. "Not without a warrant. Listen, I'm busy and have to get back to work."

"What type of work do you do?" Jordyn couldn't resist asking the question.

"Computer technician for Charock Harbour Telephone Company. I work from home." She made a point of checking her watch. “My break is over. Is there anything else?”

“Do you live here alone?” Colt asked.

“Yes. Time for you to leave. That’s enough questions.” She pivoted and marched back into her farmhouse, the screen door slamming behind her.

“Well, she’s clearly hiding something,” Colt said.

“Agreed, but do we have enough for a warrant?” Sara asked as she stepped beside Jordyn.

He sighed. “Unfortunately—”

Bones barked and tugged Jordyn to the ground.

Just as a shotgun blast echoed across the property and Sara Greer dropped to the dirt driveway.

SIXTEEN

Colt crouched and whipped out his Sig, pointing the weapon in all directions. "Jordyn, get behind the cruiser. Bones, cover!" The two scrambled to the vehicle. His heart pounded as he waited for more shots. When none came, Colt radioed for backup and an ambulance, but Greer's lifeless eyes told him it was too late. He reached over and placed two fingers on her neck, checking for a pulse. Nothing. *Lord, why?* Senseless.

The farmhouse's front door slammed, and Viv bounded down the stairs. "What happened?"

He waved at her. "Get back inside!"

Her eyes widened before obeying his command.

"Jordyn, you good?" he yelled.

"Yes. Is Sara okay?"

Still crouching, he ran over to her location, squatting beside her and Bones. "I'm afraid she's gone."

Jordyn's hand flew to her mouth but not in time

to stifle her cry. "I'm so sorry. She was such a sweetie."

"And a promising constable. I've called for backup. We need to wait here."

Jordyn slumped against the wheel well. "Why would the BoneDigger target Sara?"

Colt replayed the scene in his mind and grimaced. "Wait, Greer moved beside you. Bones tackled you, and seconds later, Greer was shot." He gathered his next words carefully. "*You* were the intended target. Not Greer."

Jordyn's lip trembled as tears formed. "She died because of me. It's my fault." She clenched Colt's arm. "This has to stop."

"I know." He squeezed her hand. "Mom told me that Linc's death wasn't my fault, and I'm telling you the same thing. You're not responsible. This is all the BoneDigger."

"Did he follow us here?"

"Possibly. Or he lives nearby and saw the police cruisers. But where did he take the shot from?" He eased himself up and surveyed the property. "I think he's gone now."

Sirens wailed in the distance.

"Help is coming. Once the officers secure the scene, I'm taking you back to your father's. I need you somewhere safe."

She stared off into space. "I'm not sure there is such a place."

Unfortunately, he had come to the same conclusion.

Hours later, Colt entered the Millers' living room and sank into the plush couch opposite Jordyn. He set Russell's two-way radio on the table—his way of keeping in touch with Ted and Oscar, who were stationed around the premises. Constable Michaels guarded the property from outside the locked gate, monitoring any suspicious traffic. Colt prayed the street would remain quiet so they could all get some much-needed rest.

Jordyn's parents had gone to bed. Colt guessed they were probably still wide awake, though, with their daughter still missing and the other in danger from a maniac bent on destroying them all.

Jordyn had retreated to the sanctuary of the warm, cozy area to read. Bones lay nestled at her feet, chomping on the bone she'd given him.

I could get used to this picture, Lord. Jordyn and Bones by his side—forever.

But he knew that wouldn't happen.

She hadn't forgiven him for breaking her heart.

And he couldn't do that to her again.

She glanced up. "Did the constables find the shooter on the property?"

He shook his head. "They scoured the region but came up empty. No shell casings either. I'm guessing the BoneDigger knows the area very well and slipped away unnoticed. Obviously a local." Colt leaned back and set his feet on the ottoman. "What are you reading?"

"I'm rereading all of Vance's reports to make sure I didn't miss anything."

"And?"

"Nothing." She tossed the papers on the end table. "We have four victims who are related. Three killed, one died from natural causes… according to the BoneDigger. What does it all mean?"

Colt rested his head back and contemplated several scenarios, then shot forward. "Wait, I remember reading about an interesting case years ago involving a family killing members of their own family. What if the three victims were generational killings? Didn't you say some were killed years ago?"

"Yes. A family of killers? That's horrifying."

He threw his hands in the air. "I don't know. Sounds unlikely—but why would someone target an entire family?"

"And let one live to die of natural causes." She picked up a teacup and sipped. "I don't get it."

"Me either." Nothing made sense about the killings. "Wait, did we get the last victim's identity yet?"

"No. It was the charred remains, so a little more challenging." She rubbed Bones's back. "This feels like old times—us relaxing in the evenings after a long day's work."

"It does. I miss it." He paused. "I miss *you*."

Her hand froze on Bones, and her eyes locked with Colt's. "Then why did you break up with me? Am I wrong, or have we reconnected over the past couple weeks? I don't buy that you fell out of love. Tell me the truth, Colt. You know I hate secrets."

It's time.

The previous conversation with his father flashed into his mind.

He got up and approached the mantel. Dare he open his heart again? If he told her the truth, he'd have to tell her all his insecurities. Was he ready to admit those?

"Come on, Colt. Please."

He turned to her and gulped in a breath.

Her eyes sparkled in the dim lighting as she waited for him to share his heart.

He sat back down, taking her hands in his. "Ever since Linc disappeared, I've struggled with all my relationships. I dated a couple times but broke it off quickly. When I met you, your beauty mesmerized me, but your intelligence did too. I fell hard—fast, even—when I didn't want to." He stopped to gather his words. "I was scared, Jordyn. Scared I'd fail you like I failed Linc. I couldn't do that to you, so I panicked and did the only thing I could think of—retreat."

"But Linc had died years before."

"You and I both know our pasts are hard to put

behind us. Mine festered for years and kept growing. You and your sister still have an estranged relationship."

She whipped her hands away and sprang off the couch. "But that's still not a good reason. We could've worked it out. Tell me the truth. There's more. What did I do wrong?"

Bones whined as if sensing the tension slicing through the room.

"Sweet Jordyn, you did nothing wrong. It's all me."

"Colt, you broke my heart. I loved you. We had even started talking about getting married and having kids."

He tensed.

"Wait… That's it, isn't it?" She sat back down. "You don't want kids?"

"It's not—"

The shriek of the residential security alarm pierced the air, cutting off his statement.

He leaped to his feet, unholstering his weapon. What had triggered the alarm? The answer came quickly…

The BoneDigger had breached the premises.

Jordyn stiffened at the high-pitched alert signaling that someone had gotten past her father's defenses. Dizziness engulfed her, and she braced herself against the couch to keep from falling.

Black spots filled her vision as she waited for the room to still. *Breathe.*

Bones barked and raced out into the hallway.

Colt grabbed the two-way radio. "Team, report. Who breached the property?"

Silence.

He pushed the button again. "Anyone?"

Nothing.

"Constable Michaels, you out there?" Colt yelled into his police-issued radio.

Tension prickled Jordyn's shoulders. "Where is everyone?"

Shuffling footfalls sounded in the corridor. Her parents entered the room.

"What's going on?" her father asked, voice booming.

"Something tripped the alarm, and I can't get in touch with your men or Constable Michaels."

Her mother hurried over to Jordyn. "You okay, dear?"

In the hallway, Bones's barking turned into menacing growls.

"Just got a little dizzy." She pointed. "Colt, go to Bones. He's alerted. We'll be fine."

"Stay here, everyone." Colt dashed from the room with his gun raised.

Her father retrieved a poker from the fireplace. "A weapon. Just in case." He took up a protective position in the living room doorway.

Jordyn helped her mother to the couch. "It's

going to be okay, Mom." Had she just lied to her mother? *Was* it going to be okay? *Where are You, God?*

Her mother patted Jordyn's hand. "I know, dear. God is in control."

"Is He, Mom? Because from where I'm standing, I struggle to find Him in all the darkness." She sat down beside her mother and rested her head on her shoulder. "Help me believe. I want to, but I've failed terribly at my faith lately."

"You were always the inquisitive one when you and Morgan were growing up. You questioned everything, but you said something incredible when you were seven. Do you remember?"

Jordyn searched the recesses of her memory but came up empty. "No. What did I say?"

"You and Morgan had been riding your bikes. She wanted to beat you to the end of the street, but she was too busy looking behind to figure out where you were, and she missed a bump in the road. Her wheel hit it, and she went flying. She skinned her knee and cried so hard. She was mad at herself for not seeing the bump." Her mother stared at the ceiling and smiled as if picturing the exact moment. "You squatted beside her and held her hand while I cleaned her wound."

"I remember that but not what I said. She always tried to outshine me." *Morgie, where are you? I want you back.*

"You said, 'Morgie, always keep your eyes

ahead, and God will shine on the bumps to protect you.'"

Jordyn had forgotten those words she'd said long ago. "But what does that have to do with anything?"

Her mother took Jordyn's hand. "You've had so many bumps and potholes in your life, love. But God has been right beside you all the time, shining His light. You've just snuffed it out. Don't be so scared of the dark, because sometimes the best things come from within our darkest places."

Jordyn's eyes filled with tears. Was that true? She had turned the light out herself and failed to see God right beside her?

Bones and Colt bounded back into the room, followed by her father's men. Ted and Oscar looked a bit unsteady.

Her father rushed to their side. "What happened? You okay?"

"We were knocked out cold," Oscar said.

"Secure the premises," her father yelled. "Now!"

The two men stumbled out of the room.

Colt handed her father an envelope. "I found this at the front entrance. It's addressed to you."

Jordyn lunged to her feet. "What about Constable Michaels?"

"He was knocked out too. He's fine, and is coordinating a search of the premises."

"This is preposterous," her father said. "How did this person get so close, undetected?"

"Good question. How well do you know your men?" Colt asked.

Her father's eyes narrowed. "I vetted them myself. They're solid."

Colt gestured toward the note. "What does it say?"

Her father ripped it open and read out loud. "'To the Honorable Russell Peters, see how close I can get to you and your family? Your fortress isn't secure. I've enclosed a gift to show you I'm serious. Confess now, or they both will die and their circle of life ends. Then you will have to live with the guilt. —BD.'"

"Dad, you need to confess," Jordyn pleaded, her pitch elevated.

"I can't."

Jordyn clenched every muscle in her body, as if in preparation to defend herself against an enemy. "Then I will never forgive you if Morgie dies."

Her father hung his head.

"Wait." Her mother grabbed her husband's arm. "What gift is he referring to?"

Russell Peters turned the envelope upside down and dumped the present into his hand.

A chunk of dark brown hair wrapped around Morgan's wedding ring.

Her mother gasped. Her knees gave way.

A question niggled in Jordyn's mind.

Had her father been the actual target of the BoneDigger all along?

* * *

A relentless buzzing filled Jordyn's restless dream as she struggled to yank her sister out of the BoneDigger's clutches. *Morgie, come on. We have to go!* Jordyn screamed, then jolted awake, realizing the buzzing sound came from her phone on the nightstand beside her. Daylight had appeared after a horrifying night. Having been assured no one was lurking on the property, they had gone to bed. Her father's fortress was once again secure.

However, Jordyn didn't believe in her father's protection any longer. He had failed his twin daughters. Jordyn recalled her last words to him before she'd headed to bed. *I will never forgive you if Morgie dies.*

The phone continued to buzz, and Jordyn snatched it up and hit Accept without looking at the screen. "Who is it?" It was six thirty in the morning—after she'd fallen asleep only two hours before—and she was frustrated.

"Sissy!"

Jordyn flung her legs over and bounded off the bed, disturbing Bones. She had to find Colt. "Morgie, where are you?"

"I don't know. She's holding me in a cold cellar."

"'She'? Who?" Jordyn hustled from the room with Bones at her heels.

"I don't know. I've never seen her face."

Jordyn banged on Colt's door. "Has she hurt you?"

"Nothing physical, but she's been drugging me."

"How did you get away?" She banged again. "Colt, wake up!"

Bones barked, scratching on the door. He obviously sensed the alarm in her voice.

"After she stuck the pill in my mouth and left, I spat it out. I was able to pick the lock with an old nail I found on the floor, then snuck out of the room and found a phone."

Seconds later, Colt appeared, rubbing his eyes. "What's going on?"

Jordyn put her cell phone on speaker. "It's Morgan! Can we trace her call?"

The news jerked him awake. He tugged Jordyn into the room and hurried to his cell phone. "Morgan, can you tell us anything you see at your location?" he asked as he typed something on his phone.

"The room appears to be some sort of old, cool storage cellar. Concrete walls."

"Where are you now?" Jordyn asked.

"In the hallway. Looks like I'm somewhere underground in an old—"

Morgan screamed, and the call dropped.

"No!" Jordyn cried. "Morgie, are you there?"

Silence.

Moments later, her phone dinged with a text message.

Play me.

A video appeared on her screen. Jordyn hit Play.

A masked man appeared behind Morgan and placed a knife at her neck. "Tell your father today is the day his sweet daughter dies. Time's up."

The screen went blank.

"No!" Jordyn crumpled to the floor.

She had failed her sister, and now Morgie would pay.

Colt paced around the dining room table as Jordyn played the video for her father and pleaded with him to confess his secret. Colt had sent the footage to Forensics, along with the landline's phone number from where Morgan had called. He prayed they'd find something useful in order to save Morgan's life and catch the BoneDigger once and for all. He was done terrorizing the community. Colt had also called his parents, asking them to pray and get all their church friends to do the same. He believed in the power of prayer.

Even though he struggled with his own abilities, he knew God's power was stronger. Always.

Fran Miller sat in the corner chair, sobbing. "Russell, you need to confess. Now," she said in between broken sobs.

Would the man finally listen? While Colt appreciated his need to protect whatever work he claimed would save lives, there had to be a way to do both. Something his father had always said to Colt and Linc popped into his mind.

Truth always wins. Every time.

Colt prayed that would be true in this case as well.

"Dad, whatever bill or work you're protecting will go on." Jordyn sat beside her mother, bringing her into a hug. "People will respect you for telling the truth."

Russell picked up the picture of his daughters as a tear glistened. "Will they, after all these years? People hate secrets."

Colt flinched. In the months he and Jordyn had dated, he'd failed to tell her about his dyslexia. He'd learned to adapt throughout his life, so why hadn't he shared it with her? Was he still ashamed of himself after all these years?

Truth always wins.

Once again, his father's words punched Colt in the gut. Yes, he had to admit everything to Jordyn. Even if it meant they'd never be together. She had a right to know why he'd broken it off.

"God will work it out, Russell," Fran said. "He always does."

"Please, Dad. You're Morgan's only hope." Jordyn's plea silenced the room.

Russell put the picture back on the mantel and turned around. "Okay. I have to call the cabinet members first."

"I'll contact Ursula Baine since I promised her the exclusive. How much time do you need?" Colt pulled out his cell phone.

"Thirty minutes." The premier exited the room.

Forty-five minutes later, Russell, Fran and Jordyn stood in front of their mantel in preparation for the conference. Russell had prepared his cabinet, and they agreed to him stepping down, promising him his work would continue.

"It's time. Shall we begin?" Ursula asked.

Russell nodded.

She turned to the cameraman. "Let's roll."

Ursula faced the live camera. "Good afternoon. I'm Ursula Baine of Charock Channel 5 News, and we're here on site with Premier Russell Peters. He has a very important announcement to make." She turned to Russell. "Premier, please tell us what's on your mind."

"Friends, I come to you today in humbleness to ask you all for your forgiveness. I didn't do something years ago that I should have, and it's time for you to know." Russell went onto confess what had happened that night, apologizing to the public and to the paralyzed man's family. He also shared the news that he was resigning as premier.

Tears ran down the stoic man's face as he finished his statement, wrapping his arms around his wife and daughter. He gazed at them before continuing, "To my family, I'm sorry I failed you.

I will live my life out trying to win back your trust and forgiveness."

"What would you like to say to the family of the injured man?" Ursula asked. "What was his name?"

Russell turned back to the camera. "To the Hickey family, I deeply regret my actions and all the heartache I caused you. I'm so sorry and pray you can one day forgive me."

Colt's neck muscles knotted as he caught the alarm on Jordyn's face.

Her father had never given them a name. What was the connection between the man Russell hit and the victims buried in the unmarked graves?

And more importantly...what was the link to the BoneDigger?

SEVENTEEN

Jordyn's heart palpitated as she waited for Ursula and her cameraman to leave after the conference ended. Colt promised to advise the reporter once they solved the BoneDigger case. However, that wasn't the reason Jordyn's heart was racing—it was the mention of the name Hickey. It had sent questions tumbling into her mind, and she could tell by Colt's bewildered expression that it also disturbed him. There must be a link. But what?

Her father's men escorted the reporter to the door, leaving the Miller family alone with Colt.

Jordyn approached her father. "Dad, you didn't tell us the man's last name was Hickey."

"I guess it slipped my mind." He wrapped his arm around his wife and kissed her forehead. "We'll get through this, love. God is on our side. I know that now." He addressed Jordyn. "Why is the name important?"

"Because four Hickeys were buried in those unmarked graves. What was his first name?"

"Jack."

She grabbed Colt's arm. "There has to be a connection."

"I agree. I'm going to the dining room to dig deeper into the Hickey family tree. Maybe something will pop out at me."

"I'll be right there. I want to talk to my parents first."

He nodded and left the room.

Jordyn inched closer to her father and took his hands in hers. "Dad, I love you. You know that, right?"

"I do, Pooh Bear. And I love you. Very much." He squeezed her hands. "I'm sorry for making you—no, *ordering* you to keep my secret. It was wrong, and I regret my actions."

"You're right. It was wrong, but I forgive you, Dad." She glanced at her mom. "The Miller family is strong, and we have to trust in each other. No matter what happens regarding your news, we stick together. Okay?"

Her cell phone buzzed with a text. She released her hands from her father's and fished the device out of her pocket. "It's him."

Touching announcement, but I've decided Morgan still has to pay.

"No!" Jordyn yelled.

Bones hopped up on all fours, standing at attention.

"Did he tell you where Morgan is?" her mother asked.

Jordyn shook her head and held the phone out to her parents.

Her mother sobbed.

Her father slammed his fist into a wall. "So it was all for nothing?"

Colt ran into the room, holding his laptop. "What's going on?"

Jordyn showed him her screen.

His jaw twitched. "I was afraid of that."

"Can you trace the text?" her mother asked.

"We tried with his first text and discovered he's using a burner phone." Colt turned his laptop toward Jordyn. "But I found something interesting." He pointed to the screen. "Look at this. Their family tree doesn't give a lot of information, but it appears that Jacob Hickey had two sons—Jonathan and Jack."

"So we have Jack, Jonathan and Jacob Hickey. A family of J's?" Jordyn's phone chimed—an alert for an incoming email.

"Yes, and somehow the BoneDigger is connected."

She logged into her email account via her cell phone and read the message. "Vance identified our last victim—Owen Hilt."

"Wait, that name sounds familiar." Colt typed on his laptop. "I'm going to do a search."

The group sat around the room, anxiously anticipating what Colt would find.

Jordyn took a position beside Colt, fighting to ignore the chaotic effect his woodsy scent had on her senses.

Colt whistled. "Here we go. Newspaper article from ten years ago about a woman pleading for the police to find her husband. He had disappeared on—" Colt hissed out a breath, slouching back on the couch.

"What is it?"

"Owen Hilt went missing the same day as Linc."

Jordyn snatched the laptop from his hands and scanned the article. "Says here she pleaded with the police to find him. She had contacted his work after her husband failed to come home for supper." She continued to read. "No way!"

Colt sprang forward. "What?"

"Apparently, Owen Hilt worked for the taxation department and had an appointment at a farmhouse on Old Harbour Road to do a tax audit. No one saw him after that." She handed the laptop back to him. "Wait, the BoneDigger said that Lincoln was just in the wrong place at the wrong time, right?"

Colt's eyes widened. "Yes. What if Linc saw Owen Hilt being killed?"

"Exactly, but my question is, why was Owen shot? That was ten years ago. Both Owen and Linc were the newest victims in those unmarked graves."

Jordyn's chest tightened, and she placed her hand over her heart, inhaling slowly.

"Good question," Colt said. "Plus, the Bone-Digger hadn't killed again until we found those graves. Or at least, that's my guess. I have to get back to the old Hickey farm. This isn't a coincidence. I want whoever killed Linc to pay for his crimes."

Jordyn closed her laptop. "Hold on… Morgan said she was in the basement of an old house. What if it's a farmhouse?"

"So Miss Winters *was* lying to us." Colt sprang to his feet and addressed her father. "We need a search warrant. Can you help expedite that?"

Her father fished out his cell phone. "I will pull some strings while I'm still premier."

"I'm coming too," Jordyn said. "Morgie will need me." Adrenaline fueled her body, giving her strength as the anticipation flowed.

Time to unearth the BoneDigger's identity.

Rain had returned with a vengeance and pelted the windshield, inhibiting Colt's visibility as he sped toward the old Hickey farm. The wipers labored to keep the view clear. After Russell had secured a judge's approval for a warrant, Colt set out with Jordyn toward the farm. Sergeant Warren had instructed him to wait for backup, but Constable Michaels just informed him that heavy rains had caused an accident, impeding his approach. The road to the old highway was now blocked. Not good.

Colt cast a quick look at Jordyn. Her tightened jaw gave her agitated state away. Her father had tried to convince her to stay behind, but she wouldn't concede. Seemed she'd inherited her stubbornness from the premier. Colt flinched. He remembered that they'd never finished their conversation. He needed to get it out…in case things went south at this farm. The dread coursing through his veins warned him the day was about to get worse. *Truth wins.* It was time.

He reached over and squeezed her shoulder. "I'm sorry to do this now, but I need to finish our conversation. Just in case something happens—"

She recoiled. "Don't say it, Colt."

"You deserve to know the truth." He withdrew his hand and gripped the steering wheel, preparing his words carefully. "Yes, I was scared I'd fail you like I did Linc, but there's another reason for me ending things." He exhaled. "You said you wanted children—and lots of them. I vowed to myself I wouldn't have kids."

"Why?"

"I have dyslexia, Jordyn. I didn't want to pass it down to them, because of the struggles I went through. My classmates bullied me in school relentlessly and called me stupid. That followed me into adulthood. I couldn't do that to a child."

She touched his arm. "Why didn't you tell me this?"

"Shame. I know that's silly. It's not something I share with people, but I've adapted to my dyslexia and proven my abilities to everyone around me, except—"

"For yourself."

Could that be true? All this time, he'd tried hard to prove his intelligence to everyone, when it was only himself he needed to prove it to? "You're right. I can't believe that didn't dawn on me until you said it."

She squeezed his arm. "I believe in you. And, Colt?"

"Yeah?"

"We would have worked hard with our children to help them. Times have changed since you were a kid." Her lips pursed, and she returned to studying the countryside. "I just wish you had trusted me with this information."

"I'm sorry. I put my shame and fears of the unknown ahead of allowing God to work it all out." And now it was too late. He'd let go of the best thing in his life—Jordyn. Now she'd never trust him again.

The farmhouse came into view, and Colt drove

up the driveway. He would find Morgan and at least give that relationship back to Jordyn.

Even if it cost him his own life.

Colt cut the engine. He hated to wait, but unless danger presented itself, he would hold back and wait for Michaels to get around the accident.

Silence halted their conversation. The only sound came from Bones panting in the back.

Smart, Colt. You did this.

But he had to tell her in case anything happened to him. He'd been wrong to break up with her. He realized that now, but was it too late for them? *Lord, I want her back in my life. Will You help me win her forgiveness?* He suppressed a sigh and observed the house in front of him, squeezing his fingers around the wheel until they hurt. *It's your fault, Colt.*

The farmhouse door opened, and a coatless Viv sprinted down the steps, flailing her arms. Her blond ponytail bounced from side to side.

Colt bristled. *The ponytail...*

Her hair had been concealed the last time they were here.

"Something's wrong. We can't wait." Jordyn bolted from the vehicle.

"Jordyn, wait for us!" *Ugh!* Why was she so stubborn? Colt shot to the back of the cruiser, opened the tailgate and released the hatch to his crate. "Bones, guard!"

His partner jumped out and bounded toward Jordyn, stepping in line with her.

"Miss Winters, what's wrong?" Colt asked as he approached the duo.

"What are you doing here again? I told you to stay off my property." She put her hands on her hips. "I don't know anything, and you don't have any cause to be here."

Colt could no longer wait. He retrieved the warrant from his coat pocket, waving it in the air. "This says differently. We have the right to search your property. Will you cooperate?"

Her eyes flashed something Colt couldn't ignore.

Evil.

He placed his hand on his weapon. "Miss Winters, I need you to—"

"Look," Jordyn whispered, angling her head in Viv's direction.

What did she see that he didn't? He looked at Jordyn quizzically, tilting his own head. *What?*

Jordyn fingered her heart-shaped necklace and wiggled her index finger toward Viv.

Realization dawned on him. She wanted him to check out Viv's pendant. Colt turned his focus back to the farmhouse owner.

He failed to subdue his gasp.

A gold-and-silver-guitar charm dangled from Viv's necklace.

Not just any guitar.

Lincoln's.

Colt would have recognized the one-of-a-kind pendant anywhere. His mother had created the design and had it specifically made for Linc on his fifteenth birthday. The guitar's body was gold, and bronze tuning pegs lined its silver neck. Linc had loved the gift and worn it every day.

Until ten years ago.

Colt inched forward. "Where did you get such an unusual necklace?"

Her hand flew to the charm. "I'm a musician. It was a gift."

"From the BoneDigger?" Colt pulled out his weapon. "That was my brother's guitar pendant, and I'm guessing there's an inscription on the back." He turned to Bones and gave the command to attack and subdue. "Bones, get 'em!"

His partner bounded toward Viv.

Her eyes widened, and she reached behind her, pulling out a Glock with her left hand.

Bones leaped at Viv, grabbing her arm in a bite and hold.

The gun went off before it slipped from her grip and fell into the dirt with a thud.

Jordyn screamed and clutched her arm.

The bullet had hit a target.

"No!" Colt yelled.

Jordyn waved at Viv. "Get her! I'm okay."

Colt bolted toward the woman, raising his weapon. "You're under arrest, Viv Winters." He yanked her free arm around her back. "Bones, out."

The dog released, and Colt cuffed the woman.

Jordyn hurried forward, stopping within inches of Viv's face. "Tell me where my sister is!"

Viv sneered. "You'll never find her. Not without my help, and that won't happen."

Jordyn clutched the blond by the neck with her uninjured hand. "Tell me and maybe Colt won't sic Bones on you again."

Bones growled.

Viv eyed the K-9. "Please don't let him hurt me."

"You have some confessing to do." Colt pushed his suspect forward. "Let's get inside out of the rain."

They entered the farmhouse and stopped in the foyer.

"Where's your living room?" Colt asked.

"To the left," Viv said.

They proceeded into the room, and Colt shoved Viv into a chair, securing her to it with handcuffs. "Okay, tell us where Morgan is." He took a peek around. They had turned the small living area into a hunter's paradise. An open barn door, hanging on hinges at the top, connected the space to a dining room, where Colt spied a wooden table.

"I don't know what you're talking about." She

focused on Jordyn. "You're bleeding all over my nice clean carpet."

Jordyn drew in a sharp breath and fell into a rocking chair, clutching her arm.

Her ashen face told Colt she needed help quickly. He scanned the room for something to stop the bleeding but saw nothing. *Think, Colt.* He noted crafter scissors on the table next to Jordyn. He picked them up and cut off a portion of his uniform shirt, then wrapped it tightly around her wound. "That should help. I have to get assistance, but I'm not sure if the roads are still blocked." He hit the talk button on his radio and gave Dispatch an update, requesting an ambulance, and also checked on Michaels's status. Dispatch informed him that the road was still blocked, but crews were working hard to clear the accident scene.

"I'll be fine. Find Morgan." Jordyn's gaze turned toward the fireplace. "Oh, my."

"What is it?" He followed the direction of her stare.

Multiple lynx paintings lined the walls.

Colt sucked in a breath.

They had indeed walked into the BoneDigger's lair.

Which meant Morgan had to be there somewhere.

A family picture caught his attention, and he moved over to the mantel to inspect it.

A burly older man stood behind a woman. A couple sat in front of them, holding a small boy. Another man stood off to the side. Was this the BoneDigger's family? Colt picked up the picture and studied it more closely. The large man rested his enormous hand on the other's shoulder. Colt hurried over to Jordyn. "Check out the size of this man and his hand."

Her eyes widened. "I know what you're thinking—and yes, a man this size could definitely crush someone's neck bones, killing them."

Colt turned the photo in Viv's direction and pointed to the older figure. "Who is this man?"

"Jacob Hickey."

"And this is his family?"

Her expression contorted with fear as she nodded.

"Why are you scared of him?" Colt asked.

"Because he was a mean old coot." Viv gnawed on her lower lip. "He strangled his own wife after she threatened to report him for abusing his grandson."

Colt pointed to the man sitting in front of Jacob in the photo. "What about him?"

"Jonathan Hickey. Just as mean as his old man. Killed his wife, too, but he paid the price of that action with his own life. My love shot him." Her expression darkened. "Right between the eyes."

Jordyn approached the dining room entrance.

"So the BoneDigger's family were generational killers?"

Viv huffed. "If that's what you want to call it. My love says his father deserved to be taken out. You see, Jonathan hated me and slapped me once. That was all it took. My sweetheart stood up for me, took his father on a hunting trip and killed him. He just wishes the old man hadn't died of old age."

"So I assume then the two women we found were your 'love's' mother and grandmother." Jordyn stood beside an end table.

"Why kill my brother?" Colt asked.

"Because he witnessed something he shouldn't have. Your dear brother just took the wrong shortcut that day."

Colt dug his fingers into his palms to curb his anger. "Owen Hilt's murder?"

"The taxman discovered my love's real identity. He rifled through tax papers and found an old receipt with the family name of Hickey. We covered it up but told the man to leave. Then my love shot him as he was getting into his car. He never knew what hit him. We had to bury my love's secret, and it was the only way to do it."

"And that's what my brother saw." *Linc, I'm so sorry I failed you and left you on the side of the road.*

Truth wins.

His father's words raced into Colt's mind once

more. He would make this family pay for Linc's death.

Colt pointed at the man standing to the side of the family in the photo. "Let me guess—this is Jack Hickey?" He set the picture back on the mantel.

"You're both too smart for your own good. And hard to kill. I tried ramming you off the road and then shooting you, but you have nine lives."

"That was you in the truck?" Colt asked.

"Yup. But now you can't escape, and you'll pay too."

"No way." Jordyn picked up a picture. "This is why she lied to us."

Bones growled, inching toward the door.

"What is it?" Colt turned his back to the foyer entrance and glanced at Jordyn.

She held up a photo. "Wedding picture of Viv and her husband. She *is* married, and look close to see who it is."

Bones barked.

Movement behind him caught Colt off guard. He turned and caught a glimpse of the BoneDigger before a shovel was slammed into his head. Recognition punched Colt in the stomach before darkness overcame him.

EIGHTEEN

"Colt!" Jordyn screamed as Colt crumpled to the floor. Kalvin Anderson, aka the BoneDigger, had snuck up behind him, catching them all unaware.

Bones barked and charged toward the man.

Kalvin raised what appeared to be a dart gun and fired.

Bones whimpered and slumped to the floor.

"No!" Jordyn hurried over and squatted by the dog's side.

"Don't worry. It's just a dart that will put him to sleep. I think I'll keep this beautiful creature. He'll help me hunt some lynxes." He bent down and removed Colt's weapon and cuff keys, then freed his wife. "Now the almighty premier will learn what it's like to mess with the Hickey family."

A shiver crawled over Jordyn's body at the menacing sound of the BoneDigger's voice. Her hands turned clammy, and she fought to keep herself from hyperventilating. *Stay calm. Keep him talking so help can arrive. Lord! Unblock the roads and save us. Please.*

She gathered strength and rose to her feet. "Tell me. Why did you change your name from Hickey to Anderson?"

"Because my father and grandfather were monsters. I wanted to rid myself of any association to them." He caressed Viv's face. "No one hurts my love or my mother and gets away with it." He turned back to Jordyn. "They had to pay, just like your father does now."

"I don't understand. When did you discover my father's part in your uncle's accident?"

"Only after you and your blasted team unearthed my graves. After I shot at you, I tried to warn you to stay away. I missed on purpose—if I had wanted you dead then, you would be. I'm an excellent marksman. Lots and lots of practice on these quiet grounds. However, you just wouldn't listen, so I began looking into you and your family." Kalvin picked up the family photo from the mantel and stared at it, pausing as if stuck in a memory. "I loved my uncle dearly. He was the only nice Hickey. We used to go fishing when I was a boy. This is the only photo I have left of my uncle, so I had to keep it." He set the picture back in its place, straightening it until it stood perfectly. He turned, his tear-filled eyes shifting to all-consuming fire. "Your father hit him and fled. Scaredy-cat!"

She almost felt sorry for the man. He'd clearly loved his uncle. "I was in the car that night. You're correct. Dad should never have left Jack, and he tried to make it right—but that has nothing to do with Morgan and me." She pointed at Colt. "Or him. Let us go."

"It's too late for that."

"How did you connect Jack's accident to my father?"

Kalvin walked to an end table and opened the drawer. He lifted out a small box. "After my uncle died recently, I was going through his things. He didn't have a wife and lived here with us after I got rid of my ungrateful father. I put the farmhouse in Viv's name, then we took care of Uncle Jack. The doctors said if he had been treated quicker, he may have been able to walk again. But no—because your father fled, and no one found Uncle Jack for hours, that didn't happen." He dug out a small envelope. "I found this in my uncle's belongings." He handed it to her. "Read it out loud."

Jordyn's fingers shook as she unfolded the piece of paper. "I'm so sorry for not stopping that night. I saw you move in my rearview mirror and knew you were alive, but I should have gotten you to a hospital. I hope you can forgive me one day. This money should help with your care. Sincerely, RHM." Jordyn gulped. Russell

Harrison Miller. "How did you guess what RHM stood for?"

"I didn't at first, but it wasn't hard after I did a deep dive into your family." His eyes narrowed. "It was then that I decided to kidnap Morgan."

Viv cleared her throat. "Well, I helped. Remember, my love?"

He kissed her cheek. "Yes, dear. Couldn't have done it without you."

Jordyn curled her hands into fists, keeping them at her sides. "You killed that witness and wounded the guard, didn't you, Viv?"

"Of course. They were in the way of my love's plan." She smiled at Kalvin. "And I put a little something in your coffee just to scare you." Her smile turned to a glare when she looked back at Jordyn. "But you wouldn't stop."

"How were you able to stay ahead of us?" Jordyn asked.

"Police scanner." Kalvin smirked. "You never know who's listening. Viv here got your cell phone records for me, too, since she works for the company. Did you like my drone? Learned how to fly him all by myself. As soon as you left my warehouse, I sent him into the air." He tapped his temple. "Smart, huh?"

Smart wasn't the word she'd use. *Monster* came to mind.

Pain stabbed at Jordyn's arm as she fought to keep strength in her limbs. She bit the inside of her mouth to distract herself and keep her focus on saving Colt, Bones and Morgan. "I'm curious about something. Kalvin, why the lynx carvings and the arrangement of the graves in a circle?"

"My father and grandfather taught me to kill on our hunting excursions. They also ingrained in me not to trust outsiders, and that our family, along with a few neighbors, formed an alliance of sorts. We gathered in each other's homes to talk about life, God and our community, forming a circle of like-minded people." He shrugged. "As for the lynx carvings…they're my favorite animal. Always skulking on their prey. Plus, they called out to me after each kill, howling and hissing in the background. I had been working on my carvings and planned to sell them at a nearby market, but when I had to move the graves, the idea came to me to add them. Seemed a fitting place."

"And the Bible verse?"

"Thought it was appropriate. They paid with their lives for their sins."

"Wait a minute. You called in the last grave we found. Why?" Jordyn asked.

"Simple. After our conversation, I knew I had to throw you offtrack. So I called in the tip, then drugged myself. I added enough to knock me out but not too much. I had to hide the needle and get back to the graveyard first."

"Why move the graves?"

"Because that insufferable funeral home

planned to steal my spot. I guess I didn't hide them as well as I thought. Someone found one and called it in. That's why I went out that night—to check on the grave." He eyed his wife. "And to get a smooch from my love. It was her in the footage. I forgot to erase the video."

Pain from the gunshot threatened to overwhelm her, but Jordyn willed her muscles to stay strong. "You're sick. Where is my sister?" She was tired of this couple's game.

Kalvin withdrew a gun from his waist and handed it to his wife. "Confiscate her phone, then take her there and get her settled. Come back to help me." He gestured toward Colt and Bones. "I'll get our other guests ready."

Jordyn stepped forward. "What are you going to do to them?"

"That's not your concern." Viv pointed the Glock at her. "Hand me your phone."

Jordyn obeyed but remained in place.

"Move or I'll shoot you right here." She gestured toward a hall. "This way."

Lord, I know I've blamed You for so many things, but please help me.

Jordyn trudged forward, passing a kitchen. "Which way?"

Viv pointed to a door.

"What's in there?" Jordyn moved closer.

"You'll see." Viv opened the door, revealing a flight of stairs going down. "After you."

Jordyn hesitated. Her elevated heartbeat and weakened legs kept her frozen at the top. She peered into the darkness.

Viv poked her in the back with the gun barrel. "Get moving. Don't you want to visit with your twin before you both die?"

Jordyn let out a cry before inhaling deeply. "I can't see the steps."

Viv flicked on a light, displaying an old basement below with concrete walls.

Dampness lingered in the air as Jordyn descended, filling her with a foreboding feeling and turning her veins to ice. A rat scurried across her path, and she almost missed a step. "What is this place?"

"A root cellar. It's where we store our vegetables, fruit and canned goods for the winter. We're old-fashioned and like to live off the land."

They reached the bottom, and Jordyn stopped.

"Keep going. Your sister is in the room on the right."

Was she? Or was Viv leading Jordyn to her death? "Why should I believe you?"

"You don't have a choice. Go!"

Jordyn stumbled forward, halting at the locked door.

Viv hauled a set of keys from her pocket and inserted one into the lock. "This is where we keep the riffraff. Seems your sister was smart enough to pick the old lock, so we changed them. This one is brand new so don't bother trying." She pushed the door open and nudged Jordyn into the darkened room.

A sliver of light glowed from a small lantern sitting on the floor beside a shelf, revealing a tiny room with a chair in one corner and—

An unconscious Morgan lying on the cot in the other.

"Morgie!" Jordyn rushed forward and dropped to her knees in front of her sister. "Wake up!"

Her sister moaned but didn't open her bruised eyes. Dried blood lined her lips.

Jordyn turned. "What did you do to her?"

"Kalvin had to teach her a lesson for trying to escape. Don't worry, she's only drugged. We had to double her dose, so she'll sleep for quite a while. When she wakes up, you two can say your goodbyes." Viv backed out of the room. "Kalvin and I have work to do. He wants to bury you-all under his wood-carving shed—a new graveyard far away from any prying eyes."

Jordyn gasped.

"Oh, don't bother screaming. No one will hear you down here." She snickered and clanged the door shut.

Locking Jordyn in a tomb with her sister.

Jordyn crawled onto the cot, snuggling beside her sister like they used to do as kids on Morgan's top bunk bed. Jordyn moved the hair out of her sister's face and settled her head on Morgan's chest. Tears flowed. "I'm sorry, Morgie, for holding on to my bitterness all these years. Can you forgive me? I forgive you and Tyler. I know now he wasn't the man for me." She drew in a ragged breath as it dawned on her. "Colt is my forever love, and I have to save him." She paused. "And you. Pepper and Ginny need their mama." Jordyn buried her face into her sister's chest and sobbed.

After a few minutes, she pushed herself into a seated position before dropping to her knees in front of the cot. She folded her hands in prayer.

"Lord, Mama told me this was her favorite way to talk to You. 'You stand tall when you're on your knees.' That's what she always said." Jordyn wiped the tears away. "Father, I'm sorry for not seeing You in the darkness. I'm sorry for all the times I got mad at You, blamed You for the evil in the world. I know now You hate it, too, and You want Your children to be a light in the darkness so others will see You." She sniffed. "I surrender everything back to You. Will You have me?" She let out a ragged breath. "I want to be that light, Lord. Show me how in whatever time I have left on this earth. I give myself to You."

Jordyn reached over and stroked Morgan's face. "Can You help me save my sister and Colt? And Bones? I love them all dearly."

She rested her head on the cot, casting her gaze toward the shelf containing canned fruit. *Lord, is there a way out of this old room?* She knew his sister escaped once. Could Jordyn find an alternate route? Houses this old held secrets. She knew that from all the tales her archeology colleagues shared.

She popped to her feet and swayed. The blood loss had depleted her energy. She floundered around the room, inspecting the walls but nothing stood out.

"Ugh!" She clenched her hands into fists as frustration overpowered her, and she shoved her shoulder into the shelf. Jars of peaches fell to the floor, exploding in the small room.

She stilled, listening for anyone approaching.

Silence greeted her, proving Viv's point that no one would hear her scream.

A mouse scooted over her feet and she jumped. "Where did you come from?" Jordyn crouched.

It was then she spied God's answer.

A gap in the wall.

Jordyn scrambled and picked up the lantern, shining it inside the hole.

The shelf had hidden a dark tunnel. Where did it lead? She returned to her sister's side and shook her shoulders. "Morgie, wake up! I think I found a way out."

Nothing.

A draft wafted into the room from the hole, making it cooler and showing Jordyn a means of escape.

But she had to trust God and leave her sister alone in order to save them all. She leaned down and kissed Morgan's forehead. "I will be back for you. I promise." A tear slipped down Jordyn's face.

She stood and wiped it away, returning to the hole. "Lord, please help this to be the way out, and keep Morgie safe." She squatted and shined the dim light.

Cobwebs and darkness greeted her. Spiders scattered in multiple directions, disturbed by the light. *Ugh!* She hated spiders. With a passion.

You've got this.

She mustered up the courage and crawled into the hole, ignoring all things creepy and crawly in order to save the people she loved.

Five minutes later, she'd reached the end. She inched out and pushed herself up, using the wall to keep her wobbly legs steady.

Jordyn raised the light and discovered she was at the other end of the basement. Could she make it back upstairs undetected? She had to try.

She extinguished the lantern and inched along the wall to the stairs. Creeping up the steps, she eased open the door and entered the hallway. Jordyn stopped, listening for any movement.

A whine sounded from the kitchen.

Bones.

But where was everyone else?

She inched around the corner, expecting to collide with Kalvin or Viv, but the room was empty.

Except for Bones trapped in a cage.

"Bones!" Jordyn hurried to his side and dropped to her knees. "I'm so glad to see you're okay."

He rose to his feet, his tail wagging. *Woof!*

"I'm here, bud. We need to get you out." She fingered the rusty lock.

Woof!

Jordyn rummaged in the kitchen drawers, searching for something to break the lock. She found a screwdriver and a meat-tenderizing mallet.

"Lord, help them not to hear this." She held her breath as she inserted the screwdriver into the lock's shackle and pounded the top using the mallet, over and over, praying the entire time.

After multiple strikes, the lock broke.

She dropped her tools and opened the door, and Bones was free.

He bounded out and licked her face.

"I'm happy to see you, too, bud. We have to find Colt."

But how?

Her arm throbbed, reminding her of Colt's shirt wrapped around her wound. He'd told her once he'd trained his dog in many areas, though primarily on protecting his charges. Would the fabric have too much of her scent on it to help? She'd have to take the chance.

She untied it, praying the bleeding would remain under control, and placed it under Bones's nose. "Sniff."

He obeyed.

"Bones, search!" Her whispered command echoed in the silent kitchen.

Bones barreled toward the front of the house, clearly intent on finding his partner.

Jordyn hurried after him, praying for strength and guidance with one thing on her mind…

Find and save the man she loved.

Colt battled to wake himself. He wanted to stop the pounding in his foggy head. Where was he? Dampness chilled his body as he willed the cloudiness to clear. *Jordyn! Bones!* He blinked his eyes open and tried to sit. Spots flashed in his vision, and he fell back down. He rubbed his eyes and attempted to study his prison, but only darkness greeted him.

And he hated total darkness.

His pulse thrashed, and he rubbed the side of his head where Kalvin Anderson had hit him with the shovel. A goose egg had formed. How long had he been unconscious? And where had they taken him? The hard surface beneath him revealed he was lying on a concrete floor.

He eased into a seated position and struggled to touch something in the dark that would give him some sort of clue as to his whereabouts.

Colt's hand bumped into a cold surface. He braced himself and used the wall to stand. Edging along the concrete, he shuffled forward, feeling as he went.

His hands hit a steel hinge. A door. He continued rubbing his hand forward until he came to the knob, turning it only to find something had braced it shut.

Figures. Kalvin wouldn't have made it easy to escape.

He pushed harder, praying it was an older door, but it wouldn't budge.

Trapped.

He slid down the door and sat, bringing his legs to his chest. *Lord, I need a way out. I have to find Jordyn and Bones before Kalvin takes his revenge out on the Miller daughters. I'm sorry for holding in my guilt all these years and not surrendering it totally to You. I give it to You now. Help me to always be honest with others and myself. I'm made in Your image, even with my dyslexia. You love me no matter what. I'm sorry for not seeing that clearly all my life.*

He rested his forehead on his bent knees. "Lord, I need Jordyn back in my life. I realize now I never should have broken it off but trusted You to work all things out like You promise. Will you give me the opportunity to tell her what she means to me?"

A tear dripped down his cheek. "Please."

A bark sounded somewhere in the distance.

He lifted his head. Was that…

The dog barked again.

Colt bolted upright, ignoring the dizziness. He pounded on the door. "Bones! I'm in here!" He banged harder. *Please, please let him hear me.* "Bones, buddy. Come!"

The barking grew louder, followed by thudding footfalls.

"In here!" he yelled.

"Colt?"

"Jordyn?" She was alive. *Thank You, Lord.* "Can you open the door?"

"There's a heavy plank holding it shut. Let me try lifting it off." She moaned and groaned. "I can't. My arm hurts too much."

Sirens wailed in the background. *Yes!* The road had been cleared, and help was approaching their location.

Shouts could be heard on the property.

"Colt! I hear Kalvin coming."

He had to get out. "Try again, Jordyn. You can do it. I know you can."

Bones barked, his claws scratching the wood.

"Okay, Lord. Give me Your strength." Jordyn's whispered prayer sailed through the door, followed by grunts. "Err…"

Slowly, the sound of wood scraping against the door filtered into the room. She was doing it. "You've got this. Keep going."

Finally, a thud—then the door creaked open.

She fell into his arms. "I'm so glad you're okay."

He held on tight. "Ditto."

Bones rubbed against his legs.

Colt ruffled his partner's ears. "You too, bud." He glanced back at the building he'd just escaped. It appeared to be a shed attached to a large workshop next to the farmhouse.

Jordyn squeezed Colt's hand. "We have to free Morgan. She's unconscious and in the basement cellar."

A click came from behind them. "You're not going anywhere."

They turned to find Kalvin aiming a shotgun directly at them, with Viv to the man's right, holding a Glock.

Fear bull-rushed Colt, sending jolts of panic through his body. How could he disarm both of them without one firing their weapon?

Sirens wailed.

Help was getting closer. But would it arrive in time?

Viv and Kalvin turned toward the driveway.

The distraction was what he needed. He flicked his hand toward Kalvin. "Bones, get 'em!"

The German shepherd obeyed his whispered command and charged at lightning speed, biting Kalvin's arm.

Kalvin howled and dropped the shotgun.

At the same time, Colt tackled Viv, sending her to the ground. He seized her gun and wrenched her arm upward. He pointed the Glock toward Kalvin. "Don't move. You're done burying people, BoneDigger."

The man sneered. "Get this dog off me."

Colt shook his head. "You killed my brother. You're not getting out of this that easily." He addressed his partner. "Bones, hold."

Bones held the man's arm in bite mode.

Two cruisers and an ambulance pulled into the driveway. Michaels, Lavigne and Sergeant Warren jumped out, racing toward them with their weapons raised. Michaels reached Kalvin first.

"Bones, out," Colt commanded.

The K-9 backed off.

"So glad to see all of you." Colt addressed his leader, "Thank you."

"Glad to help." Warren waved his gun toward Kalvin. "Michaels, you take care of our BoneDigger."

"With pleasure." Michaels cuffed Kalvin. "You guys okay, Peters?"

"We will be. Jordyn was shot in the arm." He nudged Viv toward his sergeant. "You have cuffs?"

Warren holstered his weapon and cuffed the woman. "Paramedics will check you both, okay?"

"Wait!" Jordyn stumbled forward and reached into Viv's pocket, pulling out keys. "Send them to the basement. My sister needs them more than I do. She's in the room on the right."

Lavigne held out his hand. "Give me the keys.

I'll escort them there." He hurried into the farmhouse with the paramedics.

Michaels pushed the BoneDigger toward his cruiser. "Your grave cell will be filled with concrete walls." He secured his prisoner in the back seat.

"Dr. Miller, call your dad. He's been hounding me for updates, and I'm sure he'd love to hear your voice." Sergeant Warren passed her his phone before heading to the cruiser and placing Viv into the back seat.

Colt trudged forward and pulled Jordyn into his arms. "I'm so glad you're safe. I don't know what I would have done if I lost you again." He hugged her tighter. "Can you forgive me for being so stupid?"

She leaned back from his embrace. "What are you saying?"

"I lied when I told you I didn't love you any longer. Truth is, I never stopped." He tucked a loose strand of hair behind her ear. "I love you, Dr. Jordyn Miller."

"I love you too. With all my heart." She pressed her lips on his, bringing him closer.

And stealing his breath.

Bones barked before nudging between them.

They chuckled as a cloud broke and the sun peeked its face out, finally emerging from weeks of shadows.

Colt gazed at the sky, thanking God for shining through the darkness.

EPILOGUE

Thanksgiving, one year later

Jordyn's gown swooshed as she entered the tiny white church dimly lit in the evening hour, and she breathed in the vanilla scent permeating the sanctuary. She clutched her father's arm tighter, the anticipation of marrying the man of her dreams flowing through her veins. Six months after rekindling their romance, Colt had proposed. He had brought her to her favorite restaurant, and after supper, they strolled along the water's edge with Bones by their side.

Colt chose a rock and commanded his K-9 to hop up, then kneeled beside Bones. It was then that she noticed the ring dangling from Bones's collar as it sparkled in the moonlight. The moment she said yes, Colt removed the diamond from the collar and placed it on her ring finger, then twirled her until she became dizzy. Bones circled them, barking. It was a moment that would remain etched in her memory forever.

Jordyn stole a glimpse of her maid of honor waiting in the wings. Morgan's complexion glowed in the stunning burgundy gown. Her daughters—Pepper and Ginny—bounced by her side. Their matching dresses kissed the tops of their black satin shoes. They each carried a basket of fall leaves.

Jordyn crouched in front of them. "Are you ready, my sweet girls?"

They nodded simultaneously.

She brought them both into a group hug. "Love you to the moon and back."

They giggled.

The pipe organ played a special number Jordyn had selected.

She pushed herself up and nudged them forward. "Okay, you know what to do."

They each grabbed a handful of leaves and threw them as they inched their way down the aisle, stopping to kiss their grandmother.

Morgan turned from the entrance. "I love you, Sissy, and I'm so proud of you."

The paramedics had revived Morgan a year ago in the basement of the BoneDigger's farmhouse. The twins had had a long chat in the hospital as Morgan recuperated. Jordyn had told her sister she'd finally let go of the past and forgiven both Morgan and Tyler for their indiscretion. The girls had hugged and cried as their relationship moved forward.

Ever since, they spoke every day. Jordyn thanked God for bringing her sister back to her.

Jordyn wrapped her arms around her twin. "Morgie, I love you more, but it's time for you to walk. Remember, baby steps."

Morgan laughed and proceeded down the aisle.

Jordyn positioned herself beside her father, the former Honorable Russell Miller, and secured her arm through his.

Surprisingly, the people of Newfoundland had been touched by her father's heartfelt confession. Calls poured into the media, requesting the courts be lenient on the premier. So, after much deliberation with the judge, his lawyer was able to get a reduced sentence for his crime—limited prison time along with community service. Seemed all that he'd done for their province during his years of service hadn't gone unnoticed and proved his worth. Jordyn's renewed relationship with her father had been shaky at first but grew in strength as they stayed side by side.

The BoneDigger and Viv were both found guilty and were in maximum security prisons. Colt and his parents had attended every day of Kalvin Anderson's trial, and Abigail Peters clapped when the jury announced the guilty verdict. Her older son's death had been vindicated, and they celebrated Lincoln's life at a small gathering of family and friends. They finally had closure and could move forward, stronger than ever.

Giggles brought Jordyn back to her wedding.

Morgan and her girls had reached the front of the church and were taking their positions.

The wedding march began, and the audience rose to its feet.

"It's time." Her father leaned down and kissed her cheek. "I'm so proud of the woman you've become. Love you, Pooh Bear."

"Love you, too, Dad."

The two proceeded down the aisle. Jordyn's gaze locked with Colt's, and she sucked in a breath.

Dressed in his constabulary uniform, he'd never looked more handsome. Bones sat proudly on the altar's top step, serving as best man—or best dog.

Jordyn eyed Nick and Eve, who were sitting together in the second row, holding hands. The two had started dating shortly after the BoneDigger's arrest. They were now inseparable.

Just like her and the man waiting a few yards away.

Jordyn and her father reached the front. She turned to face her dad and took his hands in hers.

The music stopped, and the pastor cleared his throat. "Who gives this woman to be married to this man?"

"Her mother and I," her father said, his voice booming throughout the church. He winked and planted a kiss on her cheek before heading to the front pew and sitting beside his wife.

Jordyn blew Fran Miller a kiss and then stepped beside her soon-to-be husband.

Colt took her hand. “You’re beautiful.”

“You look very handsome.” She fingered the guitar pendant hanging over the top of his tie in remembrance of his brother. “I love this special touch.”

“Shall we begin?” the pastor asked.

The bride and groom nodded.

Bones barked, and the crowd laughed.

After a brief ceremony and signing of the register, Colt and Jordyn approached the altar.

“I now present Mr. and Mrs. Colt Peters,” the pastor announced.

The music played as the congregation clapped.

“Kiss the bride!” her sister yelled.

The girls giggled.

Colt swept Jordyn into his arms, pressing his lips on hers in a kiss she would never forget.

Bones nudged between them, breaking them apart.

Once again, the crowd laughed.

“I love you, Mrs. Peters.”

“And I you, Mr. Peters.” Peace flowed through Jordyn at the blessings God had given her, and she would be forever grateful.

The couple proceeded down the steps and toward the front doors. Out of the corner of her eye, Jordyn caught the candles flickering in their sconces, sending a glow into the glimmering sanctuary.

A reminder of God's light shining in the darkness.

And she would shine hers brightly for all to see.

* * * * *

If you liked this story from Darlene L. Turner,
check out her previous
Love Inspired Suspense books:

Border Breach
Abducted in Alaska
Lethal Cover-Up
Safe House Exposed
Fatal Forensic Investigation
Explosive Christmas Showdown
Alaskan Avalanche Escape
Mountain Abduction Rescue

Available now from Love Inspired Suspense!

Find more great reads at
www.LoveInspired.com.

Dear Reader,

Thank you so much for reading Jordyn, Colt and Bones's story! I enjoyed diving into the world of forensic anthropology and was even able to interview a real-life Dr. Miller. She was so helpful in understanding their process. I also loved creating a fictional Newfoundland town and my version of their constabulary. This is the first book I've set in this Atlantic province, and I would love to visit the Rock one day. I've heard it's breathtaking.

Jordyn and Colt battled hardships. Jordyn struggled with being a light in a darkened world, while Colt wrestled with his own inadequacies. Thankfully, they both were able to trust God, put their pasts behind them,and forgive not only others but also themselves. God is good!

I'd love to hear from you. You can contact me through my website, www.darlenelturner.com, and also sign up for my newsletter to receive exclusive subscriber giveaways. Thanks for reading my story.

God bless,
Darlene L. Turner